WITCH SHOWDOWN IN WESTERHAM

PARANORMAL INVESTIGATION BUREAU
BOOK 19

DIONNE LISTER

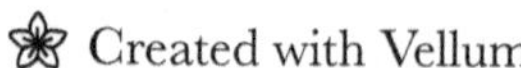 Created with Vellum

CHAPTER 1

I stared at Will, my heart a heavy bass beat vibrating in my ears. He stood at the hotel-room door and looked out of the peephole. Ma'am was out in the hall, using her talent to persuade the two non-witch Russian guards of the room opposite to help her with directions. Once they were suitably distracted, Ma'am was going to taser them. We couldn't use magic because the witch double agent in the room they were guarding would notice and slip away, and the job we'd been sent to do for MI6 would fail.

I licked my lips. Waiting. Argh. It was the worst.

Crackling came from the hallway. Will ripped the door open, and we ran into the corridor.

Ma'am stood over both men, a Taser in each of her hands. The two men in black suits writhed on the ground. Also, why did bad guys and agents always wear black suits? Was it because the blood didn't show up? I shook my head to rid it of the thought invader that would surely derail what I was supposed to be doing.

I opened the river to my magic as Will put a keycard against the hotel door. He shoved the door open, and we ran inside.

Two men sat facing each other in plush silvery-blue armchairs. The one facing us jumped to his feet as soon as he saw us. The one with his back to us jerked his head around. His wide eyes took a moment to register we were witches drawing magic, but before he could draw magic of his own, I caught him with a freeze spell. Will sprinted to him and slapped anti-magic cuffs on his wrists. I dropped my spell.

The other man's lips pinched. His gruff voice made his Russian accent even more fear-inducing. "Vot is meaning of zis?" His hand strayed to his hip. We were warned he would be carrying guns. Yep, not one gun, but possibly several. As per my instructions from Ma'am, I threw a freeze spell on Vladimir Petrov. He wasn't a witch, so Ma'am was going to have to mind wipe him when MI6 were done with him.

One of the MI6 agents who knew about my talents strode into the room. Cyril Adams, like Will and me, was wearing a black suit and white shirt. I guessed if any of us got sick of the agent life, we could transition easily into waiting tables. The tall, Black man stopped in front of the MI6 double agent. He folded his arms and peered down at Agent Barry Smythe. "You're doing this the wrong way around." Disgust curled his lip. He shook his head, then turned and grabbed a hard plastic foolscap binder folder off the table and a memory stick. He turned to me. "Please ensure you get all the photos we need. I want to make sure this is it."

"Of course."

Ma'am walked in and surveyed the scene. She turned to Agent Adams. "Your men have locked those guards in the other suite." She flicked her gaze to the frozen Russian on the couch. He mightn't be able to move, but he could hear everything. "You can question him in here, but make sure you get all the information ASAP. The less I have to mind wipe, the better. I'm also going to have to implant some memories." Her magic prickled my scalp. A plastic binder and memory stick that looked identical to what Agent Adams held appeared in her hands. She put them on the table. "When I'm done, as far as he'll remember, he'll have the information he needs. After that, Barry is going to disappear." She gave Barry a stern look. I was glad I wasn't Barry. Ma'am's death stares could strike fear into the hardest of hearts. God knew I'd suffered my share.

The Russian guy wasn't as hard to hold a freeze spell on compared to a witch, so I could afford to wait until someone told me to let up.

Barry's worried gaze found the door, and he jumped up. I opened my mouth to warn everyone, but Will was on top of it. He threw his own freeze spell on the man and addressed both Ma'am and Cyril. "I'm going to take him to MI6 headquarters. I'll see you there later."

"Good-o." Ma'am's chin rose in dismissal. She turned to Cyril. "We'll stay for the interview process. Lily can do her thing, and you do yours. I want this wrapped up in two hours. Would you like a truth spell on him?" That was usually illegal, but when you were working with MI6, legality was a formality apparently. I couldn't help smiling at my little rhyme. Angelica gazed at me, one eyebrow raised. Her look said she didn't want to know. I bit my lip and did my best serious face, which was pretty rubbish since one corner of my mouth was still quirked up.

Cyril grinned, missing our interaction. "Does an Englishman love his football? Yes, please." He cuffed the

Russian and stood over him while Ma'am cast her spell. With that done, she gave me a curt nod, and I dropped my freeze spell.

While Ma'am and Cyril got to work interrogating the Russian spy, I did my photo thing. Excitement and fear built in my belly. Once this was done, we'd have given Ma'am's boyfriend, Phillip, and MI6 their favour, and it would be time for them to reciprocate.

We were going to neutralise the directors and their criminal associates once and for all.

CHAPTER 2

Six months ago, if you'd asked me where I'd be right now, I would never have said a windowless room beneath the MI6 building in London. But here we were—Ma'am, Will, Imani, Beren, James, Millicent, Mum, Liv, Lavender, Sarah, and me. We sat around a large, black, round table, which reminded me of an American disaster movie, when the government and their advisors powwowed how they were going to stop the asteroid from hitting the earth. Angelica's beau, Phillip, as well as Agent Reece Prentice who ran the joint, and Agent Amy Plover rounded out our group.

Phillip looked at me from across the table, where he sat in the middle of his two associates. Angelica sat next to Reece, a tall, broad-shouldered blond man who could pass for a James Bond. Well, we were in an English spy agency. I assumed he was in his late thirties. His intense blue eyes seemed to see through everyone, but the crinkles at their corners suggested he might like to laugh. We'd only met him a few times, and each time, he hadn't said much. Maybe Phillip was the mouth and Reece was the eyes and ears of this operation?

Phillip smiled. "Before we start, I just wanted to thank you again, Lily, for your incredible photos. We're saving them as evidence if we ever need it."

Huh? I chewed my bottom lip. "Um, no one else is supposed to know about my talent."

He chuckled. "Ah, yes, but no one will know. If we ever need them, it will be for a trial run by non-witches, and since they could never believe something like that is an option, they'll buy that one of our talented covert agents managed to get them. We are a spy agency, after all."

Angelica looked at me. "Don't worry, dear. I've wiped off your magic signatures, and mine will fade within another couple of days. You have nothing to worry about." I gave her a grateful yet strained smile. If those photos did happen to fall into the wrong hands, no one would know it was me. Still, I couldn't help worrying about it. I'd had to be super secretive and protective of my talent for a long time. This just felt *wrong*.

I looked at Phillip. "Ah, thanks for… the thanks." Argh, how awkward.

Phillip chuckled again, and Agent Prentice's mouth curled up slightly on one corner. I was sure he was laughing at me, not with me. The lady agent just stared at me. She couldn't have been older than thirty, but her unimpressed stare rivalled Angelica's. She had straight red hair pulled into a tight pony-tail. Freckles smattered her face, but instead of making her look cute—which she might look out of uniform and with a cocktail in her hand—it made her look like more of the angry redhead cliché. To be fair, I'd met a few redheads in my life, and none of them had bad tempers. Maybe she was going to be the first?

Phillip finally had mercy on me and passed his gaze over everyone else at the table. "So, now that you've done what we asked, it's time for us to pay back the favour. As you all know, I help oversee things here, but I'm more of an overall manager." He turned his head and looked at Agent Prentice. "This man here will be running the show, as he does with all our other operations. All our senior agents report to him. I'll now hand things over to Agent Prentice."

I automatically brought my hands up and started clapping. Everyone stared at me. Imani pressed her lips together, but I saw her glistening eyeballs as she tried not to laugh. At least Liv looked sympathetic.

"Um, there was a mosquito… or a fly… or something." Or an idiot with two hands. I sighed. It had taken so long to acclimatise to the PIB, and just when I had that sorted, we had to join a new agency. Now I felt ridiculous and out of my depth all over again.

Agent Prentice, thankfully, peered around at everyone else and started talking. "I'd like to reiterate what Phillip said— thank you for helping us catch a traitor. He's been giving us grief for over a year, that we know of. He was good at what he was doing, so it was hard to prove, let alone catch him in the act. Your assistance made all the difference." He looked at Angelica and smiled. "You've got a great team."

She returned the smile. "Indeed I do. They're the best group I've ever had." As serious as everyone was trying to be, we all had small smiles. Angelica was stingy on the praise, and when she deigned to give it, it meant so much.

"Which brings me to why we're here." He ran a hand down his black lapel. "We're merging the PIB into MI6, although you might also be needed by MI5. We share information and resources from time to time, depending on what we're working on. But that's all you need to know about that." He picked up an A4 document-book thing that had been sitting on his table. It was about an inch thick and had a pale-blue cover. "This document has been signed by the relevant ministers." He grinned. "Congratulations, PIB team. You're now part of MI6, and the original directors are all fired. There'll be no more directors of the PIB."

I sucked in a breath, and I wasn't the only one. We knew this day was coming, but living it was altogether different. No. More. Directors. I smiled.

Reece turned to Angelica. "You, Ma'am, are to head up our PIB division." He handed her the document. "We can make a copy right now, and you can keep it. This one will be filed somewhere safe."

"Thank you, Agent Prentice." Angelica's magic tingled my scalp, and an identical-looking document appeared on the table. She handed the original back.

As much as Agent Prentice was supposedly experienced and versed in witches and magic, his eyes widened slightly at the copy that appeared out of seemingly nowhere. I'm sure an amateur would've looked more surprised, but the fact that he showed any reaction was telling. "Thank you." He put the original on the table in front of himself.

Will, who'd been sitting quietly next to me the whole time, cleared his throat. "Can we be more specific about what's happening with the former directors?" Excellent question.

The directors were fired, supposedly, but did they know? If they caught wind of this before we jumped on them, they'd likely disappear, which was far from ideal.

"Good question, Agent Blakesley. They haven't been informed. We didn't want to tip them off, but this starts the ball rolling in a legal sense. The rest is up to us." He glanced at

Angelica. "Ma'am and I have had time to flesh it out." He looked back at Will. "She'll have an office here, at MI6, and we're always happy to host secure meetings for your group. But for now, we want you back at PIB headquarters to arrest the traitor witches and clean the place out. Once that facility is secure, I don't see why you can't continue to operate from there. But, and I've spoken at length with Ma'am, we don't want the directors getting wind of anything until you're ready to strike at their insider agents. I understand you have proof linking some of them to the directors' activities."

Angelica watched him, her poker face intact. Had she told him about the three agents we had in the living room at her country house? They'd been there when we'd left for work this morning. We at least had proof that they were guilty of being traitors. Would they be gone when we returned home? I put up my hand.

"Yes, Miss Bianchi?"

"What will happen to those agents once we hand them over to you?"

"We'll be getting you to hold them in the PIB cells, as you're more equipped to handle a large number of captives, and you have the court system set up. If, for any reason, you can't handle the number of prisoners, we'll take the overflow. They all stand to receive life in prison. But, because of the nature of the criminals, it will all be hush-hush."

Angelica looked at me, her poker face slipping slightly as she flashed me a warning glare. When she spoke, her face had settled into its usual mask of nothingness. "In other words, dear, we go about this quietly as per usual. Understood?"

"Yes, Ma'am." Whether I understood or not, there was no other answer I was game to give. Looked like other than handing over the PIB, MI6 wasn't actually helping us with anything yet. Okay, so they'd legally given Angelica the right to call all the shots, and we didn't have to beg for funding, but were they going to offer us some extra agents to help fill the void while we trained new witch agents? Fighting the directors and rounding up their minions wasn't going to be easy or safe.

People with everything to lose were not going to go quietly.

Angelica moved her focus from me to James. "We start our clean out of the bureau tomorrow. MI6 is giving us two of their witch agents—Agents Adams and Dupont. We'll convene in the PIB conference room tomorrow at nine." What the hell? That was quick. Liv and I shared a worried look. Why were we going there of all places? Angelica must've seen my face. She raised a brow. "Anything to add, Agent Bianchi?" They were calling me an agent now because I was contracted to MI6 for the year for any special services. I'd had to sign an NDA, so I couldn't talk about anything I took photos of to anyone, not even Angelica or Will. I had a higher security clearance around here than they did, which was bloody ridiculous.

"Um, no, Ma'am." Okay, so I wasn't going to ask any questions here, but I'd bombard her when we got back to her place.

"Good." She looked at Phillip. "Back to you."

He smiled at her, the affection in his gaze clear for everyone to see. I had to give it to him—it was a brave man who loved Angelica because if you ever did her wrong, there were so many ways she could make you pay. "Thank you, Agent DuPree." He stood. "I want to thank you all for your help and reiterate that we'll be there to help you when the time comes to clear out the vermin hiding in the shadows. My guys are doing some background work as we speak, which will hopefully make our job easier when it comes time to flush them all out. If you have any concerns, please pass them onto me via Agent DuPree. And now, I have another meeting to attend. I'll see you all later."

Angelica stood, so we all followed suit. As much as this was a non-witch facility, they'd seen fit to magic it so that witches couldn't just come and go as they pleased. We had to go to a special room unless given express permission by Agent Prentice or Phillip. They had both a witch reception room and an exit room, both heavily secured, just as the normal entries and exits were. Not all MI6 agents knew we existed, and only a few were witches. That's why our group was an attractive proposition to them, I supposed. "Okay, team, meeting at my place now."

We said goodbye to Agents Prentice and Plover and made our way to the exit room. A guard stood on duty next to the heavy steel door. Each of us had to look into a retinal scanner before we were allowed to enter, the door closing and locking between each person. A light next to the door turned red when someone was inside, and when they'd disappeared, it turned green. I wasn't sure how well this would work in an emergency situation, seeing as how this was going to take ages for all of us to leave. I entered the bare room straight after James. It had a grey carpet floor, cream-coloured concrete walls, and inset downlights. No furniture, no pictures. Bare, uninviting, not a place you hung around in. Which made sense. I made my doorway and left.

As soon as I reached Angelica's, I went to her study. James, Angelica, Millicent, and Imani were already here. My questions didn't want to wait, and they came tumbling out of my mouth as soon as I walked into the elegant room. "Ma'am, do they know about our prisoners? Are they going to take them off our hands? How are we supposed to catch all the agents who are working for the directors, and how are we meant to do it tomorrow? We're not ready. And why aren't MI6 helping us more?" Did I sound panicked? Yes. Was I? Of course.

Angelica sat down behind her desk and relaxed into her butterfly-fabric chair. She focussed a calm gaze on me. "Lily, do me a favour?"

"Yes, what?"

"Breathe."

James chuckled, and I glared at him. "Don't tell me you're not worried about all this? Don't you have any questions?" Then it hit my tiny brain. "Of course you don't because you already know everything. Well, some of us mushrooms are still in the dark." I folded my arms. I was used to being one of the last to know things, but this was huge. What we were doing tomorrow could result in some of us being hurt or dying. I had no illusions about it. The double agents we were going for had nothing to lose.

Absolutely nothing.

Why did it seem like we were always heading into these situations? Because we were. What happened to the normal danger of solving crimes? I was over it. But... I couldn't be because I was contracted to MI6 for a year, and none of us could stop until the directors and their crime friends were locked up or dead. I resisted the urge to grab a chunk of my hair and pull.

"Settle, Lily." James had on his big-brother voice. "When have we not succeeded? Look, Ma'am, Will, and I have been hashing this out for the last few weeks, ever since Phillip threw his support behind us. That's what this meeting is about. Tomorrow will just be to reiterate what we're doing and deal with any last-minute questions."

"Yes, dear. As for those traitors in the lounge room, we need them. Phillip knows about them, but he hasn't told MI6.

They can go into PIB prison until they come up for trial. We're still trying to remove the spells that prevent them talking about their deals with the directors. They might die while we do that, but it's a price we're willing to pay. If we can crack it, we'll be able to untether all those agents from the directors and have them testify in court."

My eyes widened. "Wow, harsh. I mean, I know we need to, but…. As long as I don't have to accidentally kill anyone."

"Don't worry, dear. You won't be sitting in on any of that."

"Thanks." Yes, they deserved to die for what they'd done, but I didn't want to be the one who meted out justice.

"We'll get the meeting started once the others are settled." Angelica looked at the door. While we'd been talking, everyone but Sarah and my mum had come in. They finally arrived and joined us. Everyone was sitting, except them and me. I glanced around and felt self-conscious. Why was that? These people were basically family. I supposed one could feel like an idiot even in front of those they loved the most. I lowered myself into the seat next to Will. He grabbed my hand and tried to soothe me by rubbing a thumb on my palm.

Angelica drew magic and shut the door, then made a bubble of silence and called the meeting to order. "Neutralising our enemies and the directors will take a three-pronged approach. Phase one—the easiest phase—is happening tomorrow. We'll be cleaning house. The last few weeks while Lily and Will have been helping MI6 with their little double-agent problem, James, Imani, and I have been gathering all the evidence we need to try our own double agents with treason and crimes against the government. It's now time to debug headquarters, both electronically and witchily. Unfortunately, we don't have the luxury of taking our time with this. Once the directors realise what's afoot, there'll be no holding them back. They'll instruct their agents to kill first and ask questions later."

The mood in the room went from curious to sombre in the twitch of a squirrel's tail. My neck and shoulders ached from the retained tension.

"To make our job easier, I've called a meeting of all agents tomorrow in the PIB auditorium. You lot will be spaced out around the room in groups of two. You'll need to look out for each other physically as well as magically. We aren't immune to a knife in the back."

Fear did its best to edge up my throat, but I swallowed it down. We'd been through worse. I'd almost died more than once since I'd taken up with the PIB, but I was still here, and I would be after tomorrow too.

Angelica cleared her throat and magicked herself a glass of water, which she sipped, then placed on her desk. "In your pairs, I want one of you to cast a freeze spell on our double agents—you'll all be told who you're responsible for—and the other of the pair will hold a shield around you and your partner while then handcuffing the agents your partner is responsible for freezing. The only way I can see this going wrong is if we've missed a double agent. I'll be at the front of the auditorium watching for that problem." She looked at each of us in turn. "Any questions?"

Hmm, that didn't seem like a bad plan at all. I put up my hand. The look Angelica gave me was one that said if she wasn't as mature as she was, she would've rolled her eyes. "Yes, Lily?"

"What do we do with the agents once we've cuffed them, and if one of them is going to kill us, do we kill them first?"

She looked at me as if I'd just asked the dumbest questions ever. Maybe I had. "Straight to the PIB prison, of course. And yes. You will absolutely kill them if you have no choice. Obviously try not to kill all of them—we need some for trial—but if it's us or them, I don't need to explain it, surely."

I bit my bottom lip. "Um, okay. I just wanted to make sure." If I hadn't asked and killed a few, I'd probably get in trouble for being smite happy. I always found a way to get in trouble, so it was best if I asked for all the minor details first. "Oh, also, what happens if any of those agents don't show up?"

"We'll have to catch them in phase two, I'm afraid. If they haven't caught wind of what we're doing, we should have a good showing of the enemy agents. I've announced that the meeting is because of a restructure, and I'll be giving out promotions. At the very least, the directors will want the lowdown on what we're up to. Many of those agents will be there." She turned her gaze towards Will and Beren. "Any other questions?" When everyone was quiet, she gave a nod. "Good. Obviously, Liv and Kat won't be there tomorrow. I want them both here and safe." She threw my mum a smile. "The rest of you will be paired up as follows: Agents DuPree and Jawara, Agents James and Millicent Bianchi, Agents Sarah Blakesley and Lavender Belrose, and last but not least, Agents Blakesley and Bianchi."

Wow, she was still calling me an agent. I hadn't really earned the right here, at least not if you looked at all the training and experience the rest of them had. I'd skipped a few grades because my magic was powerful, but I wasn't stupid enough to think that I'd actually earned it… and nor did I want the title.

"I want each team with a maximum of four traitors, so we'll situate you in the auditorium tomorrow once everyone is seated. The MI6 agents joining us will help transport the traitors to the cells. I'll brief them tomorrow in our board meeting. Even though we haven't been spending much time at headquarters, us having a meeting will look to everyone like it's business as usual." She stood. "I think that's it for now. Go relax, lads and ladies, because tomorrow is going to be brutal."

I blinked. It was unlike Angelica to talk things up. As she walked from the room, I couldn't help but think this was all happening too fast. Didn't we need more time to prepare?

Will squeezed my hand. "Lily, look at me."

I stared into his grey-blue eyes. He was gorgeous enough to be distracting. Hmm, lucky I was easily distracted by a pretty face… or by anything, really.

"Yes?"

"It's going to be fine. We'll succeed tomorrow just as we have every other time. Do you trust me?"

I gave him a small smile. "Of course."

His magic tingled my scalp, and a plastic bag of nuts appeared in his hand. "Good. Now, what do you say we take a walk outside and visit your squirrels?"

CHAPTER 3

Let cleaning-headquarters day commence.

Will and I stood together in the hallway outside the auditorium, a list with photos of the traitor agents. Over the last few weeks, that list had grown to eighteen. Minus the three we already had, and that made fifteen we were looking out for. I glanced at the door and hoped we didn't find out the hard way that we'd missed some.

Things could get messy in there.

I gazed down the hallway. One of the rogue female agents came towards us. From the details on the list, she was forty-five, divorced, and had two children. Knowing my poker face didn't exist, I looked at Will. "You have jam on your chin." I could practically feel her getting closer.

His eyes widened. "What?" He rubbed his chin and looked at his fingers. "There's nothing there. Did I get it?"

"You pushed it to one side." I pointed to the left side of his face, the distinct sensation of Agent Fison passing my back sent shivers along my shoulders. I shuddered.

He smooshed his hand across the bottom of his face. "Is it gone?"

In my periphery, traitor Agent Melanie Fison entered the auditorium. I blew out a breath. "Sorry, there's nothing there. I was just trying to distract myself and not look suspicious." I gave him a cheesy grin.

"You what?" He shook his head. "You're a nutter."

"And?"

He grunted and gave me a deadpan look. Then his gaze moved to the list. His magic prickled my scalp, and a tick appeared next to Melanie's name. "We're waiting on two more."

The hallway was almost empty. A pair of male agents chatting to each other neared. They both said hello before going through the door. As far as we knew, they were good guys. I checked my phone for the time. "Five minutes until start time."

Will made a total bubble of silence. "Liv's watching the security cameras from Ma'am's. If any of our missing agents show up anywhere on site, she'll contact Ma'am immediately." Will, James, Imani, and Angelica were wearing earpieces today. "As soon as this goes down, if there are any missing agents, Ma'am will give us instructions. If I have to go, I want you to stick close to B. We need to make sure we all have a buddy at HQ for today."

"Will everything be okay once everyone takes the oath and passes the lie-detector spell?" Angelica was going to put everyone else through that today. With the number of agents the PIB had, it was going to last well into the night.

"It should be… at least here." Will dropped the silence spell and looked past me. I turned. One agent was coming, but it wasn't one from our list. A check of the time showed this was it. We agreed before to wait two minutes past Angelica's stated start time, then we'd go inside and lock the doors. Angelica had asked Millicent's dad to spell the auditorium so no one could travel out. We couldn't afford the power drain it would cause to our group. It would be wonderful to finally find out who we could trust and who we couldn't. Shouldering this war on our own was beyond difficult. Angelica hadn't called everyone in earlier, because she didn't want to alert the directors as to what stage we were at. She also didn't want their agents running before we could get all of them.

I bit my fingernails while we waited. It was either that or kiss Will, and since that wasn't work appropriate….

"Okay, time's up. Let's go." Will hid his thoughts behind a poker face, but surely he was as disappointed as I was. Two of the agents we'd have to go after outside, in uncontrolled conditions. "Lily? Come on." He stood at the door staring at me.

"Oops, sorry." I supposed worrying about what came later was silly because we might not all get through the next ten minutes.

I stepped into the auditorium. Will followed and locked the door. My stomach flipped. This was it. No way out until it was done. Will listened to his earpiece for a moment. "Lily, we'll take the two seats at the end of the third row down. I've highlighted what we're interested in." That was code, of course. I scanned the paper. We had four agents to look after—two in the back row, one in the row third from the back and one fourth row from the back.

Most of the seats were filled, buzzing chatter charging the room with barely contained energy—these all-in meetings weren't called often. Over two hundred and fifty agents worked at the PIB, and most of them were here. There were a handful on holidays, apparently, but none of those were under the directors' thumbs.

I made my way down the stairs to the third row from the back. Will waited for me to sit first, then took the seat next to the aisle. I gazed around the room, looking for our group. Angelica stood at the bottom of the room, behind the lectern on the stage at the front. James and Millicent were four rows back from the front on the opposite side to Will and me. Lavender and Sara were two rows behind them on our side, and Imani and Beren were in a mid-row just to the left of middle, one of the agents we were after in between them.

Well, that was cosy.

Angelica's commanding voice came out of the speaker system. "Hello, everyone. If I could have some quiet, please." She waited for the sizzle of noise to fade away. She stood tall, her shoulders back, a black-and-white pillar of strength, a woman trying to hold up the organisation she'd dedicated her life to.

I swallowed and silently vowed to be with her every step of the way.

"I'm sure you're all wondering why I've called you here today. Exciting things are afoot at the PIB, and I wanted to let everyone know about them." She did something unusual.... She smiled. I risked a glance at the baddie in our row. He stared at Angelica, his expression revealing nothing. Did he suspect anything? I bit my fingernail and slid my hand into my crossbody bag that I hadn't taken off. There were four sets of handcuffs in there. I took my job as chief smiter and hand-cuffer very seriously. Oh, crap. I'd forgotten to ask Angelica if someone else was touching a bad guy, could I still skewer them with a lightning bolt. What if it was like being electrocuted, and anyone touching the electrocutee also got electrocuted?

I shook my head and focussed on what she was saying. If I missed her signal to commence phase one, I'd be putting everyone at risk.

"We've secured funding for new recruits, and some of our loyal agents will be getting promotions. It's an exciting time for the PIB." She gazed around the room as quiet chatter erupted. I did the same. Most agents looked intrigued, even happy. One of our targets had a furrowed brow, one looked relaxed, and the others showed nothing. Maybe the directors hadn't revealed all their plans to their subordinates. How much would Angelica reveal before she gave us the signal?

Her confident voice settled the room again. "To this end, we'll be sitting down individually with each and every one of you. Everyone who wishes to stay will get a new contract. We'll have two new departments as well. One will be dedicated to spell development—we haven't coordinated that well in the past and left it up to individual agents to haphazardly do their thing. Only pooling our knowledge in this regard without consistency has hampered our efforts in fighting crime. The other department will be dedicated to incorporating animals into our work. We all know dogs are good drug detectors, but with many of us able to communicate with animals much better than non-witches can, the opportunity to have them fighting crime alongside us means we can take it much further." My mouth fell open. She hadn't mentioned that to me. I couldn't help but grin. Was my squirrel army going to be official? My smile and shoulders fell. What if she gave the reins to someone else, and I wasn't even included? Then again, nothing was stopping me from continuing with my squirrels in my own time. Whispers oscillated around the room.

Angelica placed her hands on the lectern. "Soon we'll have a bigger and better PIB, but first, we have some work to do. In a moment, a few agents will show you some things we've been working on. I'd like to ask that everyone remain seated and don't react. This is all for show." I had to hand it to her—she knew how to run a coup without causing a panic. "If my agents are ready. Squirrels!" We'd chosen that word because it made most people smile, and it was disarming in a way—when people heard "squirrels," the last thing they wanted to do was panic… unless they had a rodent phobia, but I was pretty sure none of these agents did.

I drew magic from the river as my friends' power danced like wildfire on my nape and skull. Will threw freeze spells on our four enemies. He was quick to cast, but it was near impossible to throw power-sapping spells like that simultaneously, so by the time it hit number four, he was ready for it. Or maybe he was just cluier than his mates. He threw up a return to sender. Crap. My eyes widened as Will froze.

I stared at Will for a second, but there was nothing I could do right now. Even though he'd been frozen, he'd already cast his other spells, so those three agents were held tight. Regretting our complacency, I threw up my return to sender and ran to them one by one and handcuffed them whilst trying to keep an eye on the guy who'd used his return to sender.

Agent Angus Brown was attempting to make a doorway in his aisle. If we hadn't had the no-leave spell activated, his doorway would've appeared and chopped the legs off the agent sitting next to him. Horrified, I made my way back to my aisle and excused myself as I hurried past my fellow agents. I gripped the handcuffs in my bag without showing them. I'd only have one chance. In the meantime, Will's power was draining away because he couldn't consciously access his power to stop his freeze spells.

I shot a panicked look to Angelica. But she was busy. Oh crap. My eyes widened.

An agent we hadn't accounted for faced off with her on the stage. They both wore return to senders and shields. The rogue agent, a six-foot-three battleship of a man, moved towards her. No shield would help her when it was a contest of strength. Shields were only good to stop weapons or magic, but they wouldn't necessarily stop someone strangling you, squishing the life from you.

Focus.

First things first. There was nothing I could do for Angelica right now, and she was an experienced agent. I had to trust she could defend herself until one of us was able to help her. Maybe Imani or James would be free soon. I couldn't spare the time to figure out where they were at with their traitors.

The agent I had my sights on noticed me. He glared, then hurried towards the other aisle, carelessly knocking into other agents' legs. A few choice swearwords were thrown around until Agent Brown reached the end of the row. He elicited an "Ow!" from a blonde woman. The man next to her might have been her partner because he took great exception to this. Show or no show, he didn't care. He jumped up and smashed his fist into Agent Brown's face. Wow, didn't take much to get him going. I'd have to thank him later.

I scrambled past everyone, apologising as I went—I didn't need a fist to the face. The helpful agent had surprised Brown, but now he reacted, swinging at his attacker. Thank goodness he wanted to punch on and not keep running. Made my life easier. Or maybe not.

I reached them and slid the handcuffs from my bag, but it

was impossible to click them onto a moving target. Plus, if I got too close, I was likely to get struck.

Then I had an idea.

"Sorry about this," I said to the man next to the blonde. I dropped to the ground. Their feet weren't moving as erratically as their arms. I waited for the bad guy to pivot and lift one foot. Then I shoved the handcuffs around his ankle. His other foot landed, but not close enough, so I elbowed him in the back of his knee. He went down. I scooped my free arm around his other leg and brought it close enough to shove the other handcuff around his ankle. *Click.*

He wriggled and flopped around like a fish just hauled into a boat. When he realised he wasn't going anywhere and his magic was cut off, he swore. I leaped up and looked at Will. Sweat poured off his face. Thankfully, I'd learned how to unravel freeze spells cast by others. Within forty seconds, I'd disintegrated the spell. Will bent at the waist, hands on thighs, catching his breath, his red cheeks evidence of his ordeal. He'd be weakened, holding those freeze spells for so long. But he was okay.

The agents I'd handcuffed were trying to open the door at the back and leave. I chuckled. Good luck with that. Only someone who had something to feel guilty about would do that. A normal agent would've sat there and waited for the show to be over, realising they would be freed soon.

Knowing they couldn't get away, I glanced at the stage. James and Millicent's haul must've gone more smoothly than ours because they were both on the stage, circling the rogue agent we'd missed.

I was out of handcuffs. Had anyone brought any spares? Maybe one of the normal agents here had them. The agent who'd punched Brown in the face had dragged him to the aisle, which left me a clear path. "Thanks for that. That guy wasn't part of the show. He's been doing some illegal stuff behind the PIB's back, so if you could watch him, that would be awesome." The agent stared at me, maybe trying to work out whether I was telling the truth or not. "I'm telling the truth. I'm sure Ma'am will update everyone later, but right now, that guy down there isn't part of the show either. Do you have any handcuffs on you?"

He must've decided I was legit. "No, but Agent Olsen does." He looked down at the woman whose honour he'd been avenging.

"Could I borrow those?" I smiled and looked as friendly as I could.

She shrugged. "I suppose so." She reached into her jacket and pulled some out.

I took them. "Thanks so much. I'll give them back later. Promise." It might've been good to get her help, but by the look she gave me, she still didn't quite believe me.

I bolted down the stairs to the stage, handcuffs at the ready. James noticed me first, and his ever-so-slight nod told me that it was about to go down. Angelica stood in front of the agent, whilst James and Millicent stood on either side of him. Millicent lunged in an obvious way, attracting his attention. As he eyed her, James dove in, taking out the guy's legs. I hopped around the edges of their wrestling match, looking for an opening.

James finally got the upper hand and flipped the guy onto his back, one of his arms flinging out to the side. I dropped and slapped one cuff on his wrist. He wrenched his hand free, trying to push James off him. The guy bucked and wriggled. How was I going to get those two wrists close enough together to finish the job?

Millicent solved the problem by kneeling on the agent's neck. Oooookay. It didn't take long before he went limp. Millicent hopped off him and listened for his heartbeat. She gave a thumbs up, and James cuffed the other wrist.

"Nice work." I smiled.

"Thanks, Lily," James puffed out between huge breaths.

Angelica looked back up at the room full of agents, some with worried expressions. She went to the microphone. "That wasn't a drill. If anyone else wants to admit to being a double agent, speak up now, and your punishment will be less severe than if we find out during interviews." A couple of agents gasped; the rest sat there staring. But no one spoke up. "Don't say I didn't warn you." Her firm gaze travelled the room. "Right, so, we've been infiltrated by criminal groups who tried to shut us down. We've prevailed. Thank you to all the agents who've served with integrity and loyalty. We'll need your strength and experience in the coming days as we continue to bring these criminals to justice. You'll each have a special role to play. If ever there was a time that the PIB was fighting for its life and the lives of its members, this would be that time. I'll provide more information in the coming days but ask that you be on alert at all times, both on and off duty. If you have any questions, please email them. Now, we'll call you one by one for your interviews. Thank you."

Silence enveloped the auditorium as everyone absorbed her words. She gave a nod to Will, Imani, and the two MI6 agents. It was time for them to unlock the door. Will would make a doorway to the cells, and the end of phase one would be complete. I blew out a relieved breath that we'd made it through with no losses. We'd had the advantage of surprise and executed things well. As much as I hoped the rest of our operation would go smoothly, I knew that wouldn't be the case.

We'd be facing the enemy on neutral ground, and planning could only go so far. I shivered at the implications.

"Lily, come here."

I jerked my gaze to Angelica and did as she asked. "Yes?"

"I'd like you to head up our animal training department." A smidge of a smile played on her lips.

Excitement zinged through me, and if I'd been a squirrel, I would've been doing zoomies around the room. "Are you serious?" Okay, so if I couldn't be a photographer for a living, working with squirrels and other animals was a total win.

"Whenever am I not?" She raised a brow.

"Hmm, you got me there. I would absolutely love to head up the animal training, Ma'am."

"Good. You can go home now, and we'll talk about it tomorrow." She glanced at the back of the room where the traitors were being ushered out. "I have my hands full today."

"Okay, great. Thanks." Now I just had to live long enough to enjoy my new role.

CHAPTER 4

Oh. My. Heart.

If my whole life was moving towards this one moment, it was worth it. If I never drew another breath, I would still die happy.

I stood to one side of Angelica's lounge room in the Westerham house we'd had to abandon because of enemy attacks. The nostalgia I'd drowned in when we walked through the reception-room door had been replaced by joy. We'd returned to gather my squirrels. Angelica had been true to her words of yesterday. I was going to be heading up the new animal division of the PIB, and my squirrels would be our first recruits.

Angelica, her bun and uniform immaculate, stood in the middle of the room facing her couches, which were covered by a sea of fluffy, grey fur. Thirty-six squirrels stood on their hind legs on her Chesterfields, their dark, round eyes focussed on her in rapt attention. Her magic tingled my scalp as she spoke. She was sending both words and images to her adorable audience. I bit back a smile because she looked so stern, and, well, if I didn't know better, I would assume she was a total fruit-cake, a crazy squirrel lady.

To be fair, that was actually me.

She'd just finished explaining the PIB to them and what we were doing. "So, we'd like some volunteers. You'll be working with Lily of course." She looked at me… and every tiny head turned to do the same. I couldn't help a quiet squeeeeee. I didn't want to scare them. I grinned and gave a gentle wave. A couple of them chittered. Angelica looked at them again. "You'll be relocated to the park at PIB headquarters. There's plenty of food there, lots of trees and grass, and we'll feed you as well. If anyone wants to quit and come back here at any time, that's fine. Just let Lily know. You'll be expected to work, and things will get dangerous when you're in the field."

One of the squirrels raised a paw. Angelica looked at me. "That's Grey the Brave." He was the smartest and bravest squirrel I had. I hoped he wasn't going to refuse our offer.

"Yes, Grey the Brave." Angelica said it with a straight face. I bit the inside of my cheek to prevent giggling.

Grey made a few clicky noises and a squeak, which roughly translated to, *Can I be the most important squirrel?* I smiled, and Angelica threw her gaze at me again, a question in her eyes. I nodded. "He's my most capable at this stage."

She looked at him. "Yes. But you must do as Lily tells you."

He stared at her for a moment, then chittered again. *I want to live with her, like Abby.* He didn't actually say her name, but an image of her popped into my head. "I'm cool with that." Will might not agree, but it was his bad luck. I came with baggage of the furry variety. Besides, living with people would desensi-tise him even more to us. Hmm, maybe we should allow the squirrels free rein at headquarters. Surely I could toilet train them since they understood me. We could set up litter trays around the place. Should we get them uniforms so that the agents knew they were **PIB** squirrels and not wild ones? Ooh, they could wear little suits like we did. Hmm, weapons maybe? Could they be taught to wield swords just like those memes on Facebook? I grinned.

"Lily? Lily!"

My head jerked up. Angelica's no-nonsense stare pinned me. "Oh, sorry. What?" I gave her an apologetic smile. She knew me by now, not that it made her any happier when I did float off into the ether.

She rolled her eyes. "I said, is there anything you want to say to them before they decide?"

"Ooh, yes." I stood next to Angelica and looked at my tiny troopers. I almost clapped once to get their attention, but it would've done the opposite. Well, it would've gotten their attention but only for the time it took for them to freak out and scatter. I lowered my hands calmly to my sides. Close call. I supposed that should be in their training though—expose them to sudden noises and gradually build up their tolerance.

A loud sigh came from my right. Oops. *Focus, Lily.* "Sorry, team. Right, you've heard what it entails, and I won't lie— eventually you'll be going on dangerous missions." A twang pinged my heart. I didn't want any of them to get hurt. If I was responsible for any of them dying…. Argh, maybe I shouldn't be doing this.

"Lily, are you okay?" Angelica wore her poker face, but her voice contained a hint of concern. "I know what you're think- ing, and it's too late for that. You've been trying to sell me on this idea for ages, and you did. So deal with it."

I checked my mind shield was up—yep. It was just that she knew me too well, and Angelica was, well, Ma'am. All I could do was keep them out of the thick of things, use them as distractions and for covert operations. Yes, that would work. I took a deep breath. "We'll need you for distractions and covert missions, and I'll keep you as safe as I can, but I can't guarantee you won't get hurt. So, if you're willing to live at headquarters, train most days, and sometimes be in dangerous situations, join us. As Ma'am said, if you want to quit at any time, that's fine."

A little paw went up. I couldn't hold back my smile at one of my chunkier squirrels. "Yes, Dusty?"

She made some clicks and cocked her head to one side. *Will there be lots of food, as much as we want?*

I chuckled. "Within reason. You'll have all the food you want and some extra treats sometimes, but I don't want to make you sick by giving you too much food. You'll certainly never go hungry, and in winter, you'll have warm little squirrel houses to live in."

Angelica raised a brow. "Is that so?"

I shrugged. "Why not? It's not like it'll be that much work to make some comfortable boxes for them in the trees with bedding. We could even have a squirrel door so they can come into the building whenever they want. Once they're toilet trained, maybe we could have some inside accommodation for them?"

She stared at me for a few beats. "If you mollycoddle them too much, they'll lose their… edge." The look on her face told me she couldn't believe she was having this conversation. Besides, how much *edge* did a squirrel have?

I blew out a breath. "Can we talk about this later?"

She waved a dismissive hand. "Can we just get this over with, dear?"

Why couldn't she just be not difficult for once? I looked at my potential squirrel army again. "Anyway, you'll at least have nice little shelters in the trees, plenty to eat, and you get to help us put mean witches in gaol so they can't hurt others." They had everything they needed in Angelica's backyard and the reserve behind us. Suddenly this didn't feel like such a great idea. They were giving me their time and effort for maybe nothing. "Um, look, if you don't feel you're getting much by agreeing, that's fine. I understand."

Grey the Brave put up his hand and chittered, his clicking quite loud. *We like you, Lily. The things we do with you are fun.* Did they even have a concept of good and evil, or was it just about survival with no intent? Was I forcing our way of looking at the world onto them to their detriment? Was it akin to asking a five-year-old to work for us?

"Um, do you know there are bad people, and we want to stop them hurting others?" I sent emotions and images their way.

A few of them nodded. My mouth dropped open. Since when could they do that? Grey communicated again. *Most of us understand. You've kept us safe, and we want to do the same for you. We know you're good.*

These gorgeous little creatures. I didn't deserve their loyalty, but I was going to take it anyway. Argh. I was such a bad witch. "Okay, then. All the squirrels who want to come with me, please stand behind me. All the rest, stay where you are." I held my breath as they decided. How many would come across?

Grey the Brave was the first to jump down. Others followed him, leaping to the floor and scurrying behind me. Of the thirty-six squirrels we started with, only eight remained on the couch. I smiled at the ones who chose to stay here— eight less I'd have to worry about. *Remind me again why you thought this was a good idea?* "I'll make sure we still drop food by every now and then. Hopefully, we'll move back here soon anyway, so I can see you more often. I won't forget you. I guess you can go." A couple sent thanks my way as they all bounded off the couch and out the door.

I turned and looked down. Twenty-eight furry little faces gazed up at me, front paws touching in front of their chests. I was relieved that Dusty was one of them. Well, relieved and worried. I guessed I just needed to make sure I trained them so well that they couldn't help but survive. "Thank you all for sticking with me and helping. Is everyone ready to go?"

Lots of little yesses filtered into my brain. Eek, it was time to start my program.

I grinned at Angelica. One corner of her mouth curled up. Ha! Even she wasn't immune to their cuteness and this whole crazy situation. I smiled down at my charges. *I promise to keep you all as safe as I can.* It was time to get this thing happening.

"Okay, Team Turmoil, so this is how a doorway works…."

Let the chaos begin.

CHAPTER 5

I stood in the large parklike grounds that surrounded headquarters and pointed halfway up a large oak, its bright-green canopy healthy and lush. "I think the last one can go up there. Is that good, GTB?" I'd taken to calling Grey the Brave by his initials because his name was way too long, and since most of my squirrels were grey, it would get confusing. He sent back feelings of happiness.

Beren chuckled. "Okay." His magic tingled my scalp, and the premade timber squirrel house disappeared from his hands and appeared at the juncture of a branch and the trunk. The nails in Beren's palm disappeared. After a moment, his magic stopped. "Done. Twenty squirrel lodgings situated. That should keep them happy. How many squirrels do you plan on recruiting?"

"I have no idea. I guess a few more would be good. Maybe some of the ones who already live around here would like to join?" I'd been feeding some of them for a while, well, when I was here before. Since all this director stuff had happened, I hadn't been here much because Angelica had wanted to keep us safe. I missed her house too. The sooner we could squash the baddies, the sooner we could go home. It had been way too long since I'd walked from her place to Costa and enjoyed my cappuccino and double-chocolate muffin. The directors had someone watching the place all the time because they knew I liked going there. Crapheads.

"Well, let me know if you need more houses, but I'm sure the ones that came from Angelica's hang out together, so they probably won't use every house."

"Thanks, B. You're the best." I smiled. I had the most incredible group of friends a person could wish for.

He tipped his pretend hat. "Happy to be of service, m'lady. So, when do you start teaching them stuff?"

"Well, I've only just shown them around, so I figured I'd give them a day to get used to the place, and tomorrow, we'll start." My phone rang, as did Beren's. We looked at each other, my worry mirrored on his face. We took our phones out of our pockets and answered in unison. "Imani, what's up?" Beren had walked a bit away so our conversations didn't clash.

"Meeting now in the conference room."

"Cool. Be there in a couple of minutes."

"Bye." I looked down at GTB who hadn't run off to look at his home yet. I'd had a chat to him, and we'd agreed that he'd sometimes live with me and sometimes here. I didn't want him to lose touch or influence with his squirrel family. I'd also taken Angelica's comment about "losing their edge" seriously. "I have to go now, but I'll be back later." He stared at me, his big eyes intense, but no message came through.

Beren got off the phone. "Did you get called to the conference room as well?"

"Yep. Let's go." Angelica had told us to be wary at HQ

for a while, until we were sure there were no double agents left, which had me staring at the agents we passed as we made our way to the conference room. Everyone was side-eying everyone else. Fun times. Yesterday's interviews had uncovered two more we didn't know about, but everyone else had retaken their oaths and had promised upon death that they weren't involved with the directors in any way, shape, or form.

Beren opened the conference-room door for me, and I went in first. Looked like we were the last to arrive. As well as our group, two MI6 agents were there—the non-witch Amy Plover, and the witch Cyril Adams, plus an agent I didn't know. The man looked to be in his late forties or early fifties. His short grey hair framed a kind-looking, clean-shaven face. Was he PIB or MI6? We all had similar uniforms, so there was no clue there. I snuck a look at his aura, and he was a witch. Hmm, probably PIB.

I took the empty seat opposite Will and in between Milli-cent and Liv. Beren took the last seat next to Cyril.

Angelica's magic tickled my scalp as she made a bubble of silence. "Thank you for getting here on short notice."

My eyes widened, and I jumped in my seat as something pricked my leg. I pushed my chair out and looked down. Oh dear. GTB climbed up my leg and settled in my lap. He looked at me as if to say *what*?

"Lily, what in the seven hells is going on now?" Angelica stared at me. She leaned forward, her gaze landing in my lap. "Why is there a squirrel on your lap?" Everyone stared at me, and my cheeks heated.

"Um, your guess is as good as mine."

Will smirked, and Liv pressed her lips together, holding in a smile. Angelica shook her head. "We don't have time for this.

Let's just continue." Right, well, I wasn't the one who stopped the meeting to scold me.

GTB chittered quietly, his message floating into my head. *Sorry for getting you in trouble.*

Aw, so adorable. I thought back to him, *That's okay. Angelica's usually cranky. It's not your fault.* I looked up. Phew. No one else had heard that. Only Will and I could talk to each other mind to mind, at least as far as I knew, but animals seemed to have that ability. Interesting. I leaned to the side and whispered to Imani, "Did you hear what GTB just said?"

Her nose crinkled. "Who?"

"The squirrel. He spoke to me in my head."

"No, love, I didn't." Hmm, they could probably control who heard them then. That was pretty amazing.

Angelica's voice held a note of annoyance. Okay, it was more like a symphony. "Am I interrupting, Lily?"

Gah, I hated meetings. I sighed. "No, Ma'am. Please continue."

She raised a brow. "Another interruption, and you can leave." Ooh, she wasn't playing. Agent Plover gave me a dirty look. Ooookay. Up yours, too, Judgy Mcjudgeface. She was probably wondering what the hell I was doing here.

You and me both, lady.

"Yes, Ma'am." Should I interrupt so I could go? I could take GTB to the cafeteria and share a chocolate muffin. It would probably be bad for him, but just a crumb couldn't hurt, could it? Imani, probably sensing I was again off with the fairies, subtly elbowed me without taking her eyes off Ma'am.

"After yesterday's operation, we now have agents we can trust. I know everyone's still on edge, but I can assure you that we've weeded the traitors out. Because the situation with phases two and three is pressing and will take resources, I've appointed another agent to manage local cases. Please welcome Agent Barney Link to the team." She smiled at the grey-haired agent.

He returned her smile and held up his hand in a hello gesture. "Lovely to meet you all." He looked at Angelica. "Thank you for the privilege of overseeing our local cases, Ma'am. I promise to do you proud and lighten your load so you can concentrate on taking these scum down."

Her smile widened. I hadn't seen her this happy since… well… since never. Okay, I lied. She smiled and even laughed at Will's and my engagement. "Thank you, Agent Link. I trust you'll do just that. This is my team." She introduced us one by one. At least Agent Link seemed like a happy, easy-going fellow. One grump in charge was enough.

Agent Link looked at me. "Lily, I heard you were heading up a new animal training division for us. When you've got a minute, I'd love it if you could run through it with me. I have some ideas for how we can utilise the new resources, and my ideas might inform your training. Would that be okay?"

I smiled. Polite and cordial. Mmm, cordial. Come to think of it, I was thirsty. The last time I'd had cordial was maybe five years ago. How sad. I'd have to rectify that soon. A weight pushed into my stomach. I looked down. GTB had climbed to there and was pulling at my shirt. *Pay attention.* Oh dear. You knew things were bad when a squirrel was telling you to concentrate. I gazed across the table at the man whose eyes glimmered with humour. "Of course, Agent Link. That would be great. Just tell me when, and I'm there."

Angelica leaned forward. "Good. Now that's settled, we have a lot more business to discuss."

Agent Link winked at me. I grinned. We were going to get along just fine. Angelica gave me a look that suggested she wasn't impressed, but Agent Link escaped the same fate. Lucky man.

"Phase two commences today. We considered trying to meet with them to call them off the attack, but they have too much to lose, and we can't give them ongoing immunity from arrest, so we thought best just fight this fight now and get rid of as many as we can. In most cases with these organisations, if you cut off the head, the tail flops around aimlessly, then dies. This is what we propose." Her magic tingled my scalp, and an A4 booklet appeared in front of each of us. "We've identified every person we need to arrest or eliminate." She stared at us, her eyes intense, grave. "I want you all to learn those faces, names, talents by heart. In two days, we'll meet here again and strategise. My plan is to take out the two more powerful crime groups first and hope that the third one slinks away into the night when they realise what's happening. Once they're taken care of, we go for the directors. And this is where MI6 comes in." She looked at the two agents. "They've uncovered the directors' secret hideaways so we should be able to find them if they run. That doesn't mean we know everything, but hopefully, we've got most of what we need. Without the crime gangs protecting them, apart from their magic, they should be easy enough to corral." I put up my hand. "Yes, Lily?"

"Won't the crime gangs be less likely to fight us once they know the directors hold no sway? Why would they risk themselves when there's no more benefit?"

She sipped her water and placed it back on the table. "Two reasons. One: the directors would have lots of information on them that they could make available to the police, us, and MI5 with an email. If the directors are going down, they're taking them all with them. Secondly, they would've gotten them to swear an oath as they did for the agents. There's always a price." Her gaze moved around the table. "Any other questions?" No one said anything. "Good. So, read up on our enemies, and get ready. Be on your guard at all times, especially outside this compound. By now, the directors know they've lost control, and we don't know what lengths they'll go to avoid capture. Assume the worst." She stood. "Dismissed."

Wow, that wasn't ominous. Not at all. I found myself stroking GTB. So soothing. "You're soooo soft." He made a little sigh. Despite the reminder of danger we'd been given, happiness warmed my chest. A wild, warm, soft little creature was trusting me enough to sit in my lap. As far as memorable moments went, not much beat this.

Across the table, Agent Link stood. "Lily, why don't we have that meeting now. I've got a lot on this afternoon, and I think the earlier you know what we need from these critters, the better."

"Okay, sure." I put GTB on my shoulder and stood.

Will came over and smirked at my companion. "So, you're like a pirate but on land, and your parrot is a squirrel. Captain Lily."

I chuckled. "Seems like it. I don't think this will be an all-the-time thing. Maybe he's just nervous about being in a new place?"

GTB squeaked and chittered. *I want to go where you go. Can I be second in charge now that the cat isn't here? I won't cause any trouble. Promise.*

Will's eyes widened. So, he heard too. I bit my bottom lip, thinking. "Um, I guess so, but you'll still have to stay in the park here sometimes—your friends and squirrel family are here."

I suppose so. Can I come with you when you talk to Agent Link?

"Okay. I guess that'll be okay." Just when I thought I'd seen everything with my squirrels, one turned out to have the brain of a human. I wasn't sure if that was a good thing or a bad one.

Thank you.

Will wrinkled his forehead. "Wow, Lily. I think you'll have your work cut out for you. Grey the Brave is going to give you a run for your money."

Angelica had quietly come to stand next to me, her expression as deadpan as they came. "Now you'll know how I feel dealing with you, dear."

I rolled my eyes. "The difference being that I don't ask to go everywhere with you. If the universe would just give me a break, I'd be off taking landscape photos instead of taking out bad guys."

Agent Link made it around to my side of the table. "Come on, Lily. Let's get you and your little friend away from these meanies." Angelica kept a straight face, but there was no tension coming off her. How did this guy get away with it? Maybe he'd proven himself to her over the years, and she had a soft spot for him.

"Okay." Despite the attention because of GTB, I didn't miss the looks the MI6 female agent gave me. Her expression morphed between disgust and confusion. Maybe she wondered what the hell I was doing here because I made the PIB seem pathetic. And maybe she was dreading working with me. As I followed Agent Link out, I couldn't help but feel the same… about all of it.

CHAPTER 6

I spent the afternoon training squirrels. The first order of the day was to get them toilet trained. So now they knew to hold on till they were outside, or they had to go to the kitty litter trays I'd had placed throughout HQ. They were discreet, enclosed ones spelled to keep clean. The next thing I'd done was give them names and made sure they knew what they were. We were still working on that one. Just over half my squirrels came when I called their name. I'd get the slower ones perfecting that tomorrow, and then the real training could begin. I was just saying goodbye to the squirrels in the HQ park when my phone rang. It was a number I didn't recognise. I got ready to hang up if it was a scammer.

"Hello?"

"Hello. Is that Lily Bianchi?" a vaguely familiar English-accented voice asked.

"Who wants to know?" With all the drama we'd had, I wasn't just giving up everything to the first stranger who called.

"It's Agent Reece Prentice." Oh, the MI6 guy.

"Hello, Agent Prentice. What can I do for you?" Argh, I didn't want to ask that question, but I had to help them for the next twelve months as per the agreement that Angelica and Phillip negotiated. The things I did for my friends.

"We need your help with something. I was hoping you could come to MI6 HQ now if you're not in the middle of anything." Their phone calls were probably scrambled so no one could listen in, but best that he kept things vague. I'd find out what it was about when I went there.

"Okay. I'll be there in a couple of minutes. See you then."

He chuckled. "Give me five. I have to make my way to the reception room."

I smiled, not that he could see it. "Yeah, sure. See you soon." We hung up, and I called Angelica and told her I'd been called in.

"Okay, dear. Just do your best, and if you're concerned they're asking you to do something dangerous, let me know. If I need to, I'll send someone to watch out for you."

I appreciated that she worried about me, but wasn't I an experienced witch now? Didn't she call me when she needed help? "Okay, thanks. Bye." One minute I was capable and amazing, the next I was in need of protection and coddling. No wonder my confidence was all over the place at times.

I remembered the coordinates for MI6 headquarters, stuck them on my door, then walked through. As I stepped out into the stark, white room that contained four chairs and a water cooler, I hugged myself. This was the first time I'd been here by myself. The people in this place were almost all strangers. Yes, this was a government organisation, so you'd think I could trust them, but after watching too many conspiracy movies, I was nervous. They didn't have a vested interest in my safety. They could easily ask me to take photos somewhere that I would be more vulnerable to the PIB's enemies. What if there was a mole here, and they tipped them off as to where I'd be? As Angelica had warned this morning, I needed to be on my guard at all times.

I made a return to sender and buzzed the intercom. A guy in a guard's uniform opened the door, Agent Prentice walking up to us as I exited. "Ah, great timing, Agent Bianchi."

I bit my tongue to keep from saying I wasn't an agent and just call me Lily. Maybe the agent thing would give me a bit of respect here. Now, if I could just not act like an idiot for however long this job took, I might deserve the title. "What's the job you need me for?"

He gave the guard a pointed look, then turned back to me. "I'll tell you in my office. Come on." His broad-shouldered, black-suited form cut an imposing figure as he led me down a marble-floored hallway, his shiny black dress shoes echoing quietly with each step. If I didn't know he ran the joint, I would've assumed he held some kind of important position. Even so, he didn't seem arrogant so far, and not nearly as stern as Angelica. My nerves went from a ten to a wavering seven.

We took the lift to the top floor. Down another corridor, we finally came to a closed door, much the same as the other closed doors we'd passed. He opened it and ushered me in.

Whatever I'd expected, this wasn't it.

Rather than being macho and clinical, the room was more like a cosy study you'd expect to find in a country estate—and I say estate rather than house because the things in this room were opulent, elegant, and definitely expensive.

A blue-and-white Persian rug covered most of the herring-bone timber floor. His timber desk—a plush, leather, high-backed chair behind it—sat under a large window. To one side was a fireplace with two oversized eggshell-blue armchairs and an antique round table between them. Another dark timber semi-circular table cosied up to one wall, two photos and an antique clock sitting on it. The other side of the room contained bookshelves, which were jampacked with books and knickknacks. A picture of Queen Elizabeth with her corgis hung on the wall near the door. Other pictures were propped up on his desk, but they faced the other way, so I couldn't see what they were.

He pulled his chair out and gestured to one of the black leather guest chairs facing his desk. "Please, sit. Can I get you something to drink?" With his accent, I couldn't help thinking of James Bond. Hmm, should I order a martini? I suppressed a giggle.

Argh, at least try and act like a professional. "Um, no thanks. I'm fine." Maybe next time. "So, what do you need?"

"One of our agents has gone missing in Monte Carlo." He handed me a headshot of a pretty woman in a black jacket and white shirt. She would've been in her late twenties or early thirties. "She's been missing for a few days. We were hoping she'd turn up, but all traces of her are gone. Her phone is off grid as well. With no security footage and no evidence of her ever having left her hotel, we've come to a dead end. Your photos were what got us over the line with the other case. It's also why we've contracted you for a year. I need you to fly to Monte Carlo with one of my agents and take some photos in the hotel room Agent Riverbed was booked into."

I handed the picture back. "I can probably travel your agent there. We could be there in minutes." I wasn't up to date on where all the public-toilet landing spots were, but surely there'd be quite a few.

He stared at me for a while and rubbed his jaw. "That's not our usual way of doing things."

"Ah, okay. I just thought it would save you time and money, but if you don't want to… no worries." I knew they didn't have many witches on staff, and not all the agents knew about witches, but they had witch reception rooms. Stands to reason they should travel sometimes. Apparently my reasoning wasn't cutting it.

He rested his hands on the table and linked them. "It's not that it's not a good idea. We don't have many witches on staff, so we don't ask them to ferry other agents to and fro. We tried once, and the witches involved threatened to quit because they felt like chauffeurs. Plus, we have so many agents needing to travel, that it took them out of circulation. Also, we don't want our non-witch agents to get used to the easy way. It messes with their mental toughness, not to mention, keeping it under wraps from agents not yet sworn to secrecy and aware of witches…." If we were partnering with them more closely in the future, surely they'd have to remedy that situation and educate all their agents?

I opened my mouth to argue that it didn't mess with the mental toughness of PIB agents, but that wasn't why I was here. "What about just this once, since it's me, and I don't mind. In fact, I'd rather transport someone than spend hours commuting. Just let the agent know it's a one-time thing. I'm sure your missing agent would appreciate us being hasty." If she wasn't already dead.

"You make some good points." He pressed his lips together. "Fine. You can transport them there. While you're there, I want you finding out if there was anyone else in their room at any time they were there. Find if there's any classified information. Find out what state they were in the last time they were there, etcetera." *If they were dead, how they were killed.* Why wouldn't he just say it? Was the head of MI6 superstitious, or was it a general thing with non-witch agents?

"Got it. I'll get all the evidence I can. I take it the agent I'm going with is one of the few who know about my talent?"

"No, so be discreet. As far as they're aware, you're looking for evidence and taking photos, but they won't know exactly where you fit in. That's normal for how we operate. Everyone has secrets here, secrets about themselves or about the job they're doing or have done. It's how it has to be."

"Ah, right. Is that code for don't ask questions?"

He smiled. "I'm glad you understand." He handed me a piece of paper. "That's the hotel and room number. Also, the agent's name is Agent Riverbed. I know you, ah, need to ask your… magic specific questions." Hmm, Riverbed. Another made-up name. They couldn't all be 007, I supposed.

I smiled at how awkward he was. If you weren't used to talking about magic, it was totally weird. Goodness knew I was in shock for the first few weeks of realising these things existed. But they did have a few witch agents. From what I'd seen, though, they didn't like to use them or talk about it. Hence why Phillip wanted the PIB more involved here. Phillip must have kept his skills to himself most of the time. "Yes. Thanks for that." I held the paper since I'd be using it soon.

Prentice picked up the receiver of the phone on his desk and pressed a button. "Send Agent Sunshine in, please." Agent Sunshine? Was that a proper name or made up? I was about to ask when I remembered—don't ask, don't tell. Fine. I was the worst person to have here. How was I supposed to have a conversation without letting something slip? And how was I going to keep my natural curiosity tamed? This job was going to drive me nuts, and just when I thought I couldn't get any crazier than being a squirrel trainer.

The door opened, and I turned in my seat. A huge Black man walked in. He had to be at least six five and was built, as we say in Aussieland, like a brick, ahem… "number-two" house. He must hit the gym every day. He looked to be in his early thirties, and his hair was ultra-short. His gaze flicked to me before bouncing off and going straight to Agent Prentice. He sat.

Agent Prentice looked at me. "Agent Bianchi, meet your partner on this mission, Agent Sunshine. Agent Sunshine, meet Agent Bianchi."

The huge man turned in his seat and offered his hand. I shook it, my hand like a five-year-old's in his massive grasp. "Lovely to meet you, Agent Sunshine."

"Likewise." His deep voice sounded like tightly coiled energy and strength and could probably stop people in their tracks, even with a whisper. He might not be a witch, but he had powers of intimidation—the way he sat and loomed, and the ominous vibration of his voice. He turned back to Prentice.

"Your assignment today is to keep Agent Bianchi safe. I don't know if the room is bugged or if anyone's watching. Just be careful and let Agent Bianchi do her thing. Then come straight back. Is that understood?"

"Yes, sir."

I followed Sunshine's lead. "Yes, sir." Sounded simple enough.

Prentice handed Sunshine a keycard. "This is to get into the room." He paused and licked his lips. "You'll be getting there an unconventional way. I don't need to tell you that this is confidential and comes under your NDA. Also, don't get used to it. This is a one-off."

Sunshine didn't so much as flinch. It was as if Prentice had just told him he'd be serving tea and scones in the dining room. Mmm, tea and scones. My stomach gurgled. Damn not eating for four hours. It was too late now. Maybe I could pick something up in Monte Carlo before we returned. "Yes, sir. Is that all, sir?"

"Yes, Agent Sunshine. Dismissed." He gave us a nod, and Sunshine and I stood.

As we walked out, I asked, "Do you know the way to the exit room? I've only been here a couple of times, and I've never been to this part. I have no idea where I'm going."

He gave me a look that said if you can't even find your way around here, how are you going to get us to Monte Carlo? Or maybe I was just paranoid. "Follow me. That room doesn't get used much. I don't even know why they have it."

I tried to memorise the route as we went—one day I might need to find my way by myself or in a hurry for my own safety. We reached the room within a couple of minutes. The guard standing outside the door asked us to scan our IDs. For a room they hardly used, they had a guard next to it. Maybe they used it more than Agent Sunshine realised. Maybe the witches coming and going wore no-notice spells. Hmm. How much did Prentice and his non-witch buddies know about witches? Maybe I shouldn't let on about all the stuff I could do. Maybe we'd keep it to travelling and for a select few, my photo talent. For all his strength and likely skill at killing people, Agent Sunshine was still just a human with no magical skills. I could freeze him in an instant. My shoulders relaxed as the guard locked the door after us.

Without getting cocky, I needed to remember that I was powerful and capable, even if people around me didn't see me that way. I thought back to when I saved us from that house where we almost blew up and how far I'd come over the last year. I smiled to myself. *Don't forget it, Lily.*

I checked the address on my piece of paper, drew on my magic to bring up the witchy map in my head, and pinpointed where the closest public toilet was. I smiled. In a park right across the road. Nice. I turned to Agent Sunshine. "When you walk through the doorway I'm going to make, don't touch the sides, or you'll lose whatever piece of your body it is. It kind of chops it off."

He looked at me, assessing.

"I'm not kidding. When we step through, we'll come out in a public toilet. Just get out of there because I'll be walking in behind you, and you'll be in my way. It's across the road from the hotel we're going to."

He stared at me, possibly still trying to work it out—was she lying or telling the truth? I guessed he'd have to find out for himself.

I drew my magic, created my doorway—taller than normal to make sure I didn't shave off the top of his head—and stuck the coordinates on. It shimmered in the stark exit room. I motioned him to step through. "You go first." If he lost the plot, I'd have to fix things, and if I disappeared in front of him, he might, I didn't know, freak out? Also, once the doorways were created and the owner stepped through, unless you made a special effort to keep it open, it closed automatically. That would also be a problem. Then I'd have to travel back to MI6 and the reception room, then back to the exit room. I was tired just thinking about it.

He narrowed his eyes but then shrugged and stepped forward, into the shimmer. Once he was through and gone for long enough that I'd given him time to get over any shock and move, I went through. The cubicle door bounced shut—I'd only just given him enough time. I opened it and made my way outside. Agent Sunshine's back was to me when I exited into the lush, green park. He turned and stared at me. Was that awe on his previously unimpressed mug? "I… how?"

I smiled. It was nice not to be the clueless one for a change. "Magic." I shrugged. "I don't know how it works, but it's pretty amazing, hey."

"I'll say." He peered around. "And this is definitely Monte Carlo. I've been here so many times. If I hadn't experienced it myself…."

"Have you ever seen any witches doing their thing?"

"Nope. First time. What else can you do?"

"A bit of this, a bit of that." I grinned. "It's particularly helpful for cleaning the house in two seconds too." I wasn't going to spill all my secrets. The more everyone else knew about what we could do, the fewer advantages we'd have. Plus, I didn't want him to be scared of me. I wasn't about to tell him I could smite people with lightning… or read minds. That's when crap would get real. It was one of the reasons non-witches would want to go back to the olden days of burning witches at the stake or weighing them down with rocks to sink to the bottom of the river. Fear made people capable of horrible things. "Anyway, we'd best get going."

Just so we didn't end up being confronted, I put a no-notice spell on both of us without telling him. He wouldn't know any different, and since he had the keycard to the room, we wouldn't have to ask anyone for it.

The hotel wasn't that impressive, to be honest. I'd been expecting the glitz and glamour of James Bond since this was MI6, but the building was a multi-level, rendered-brick affair, probably built or at least renovated in the 1990s. At least they weren't wasting taxpayer money on living the high life.

Glancing around to see if we were being watched, I followed Sunshine to the lifts. When we got in, he swiped the keycard to the fourth floor. So far, so good. There didn't seem to be anyone spying or following, and if we were dealing with non-witches, my no-notice spell would have thrown them off. But the room might be a different story. They were probably waiting for MI6 to come searching for their lost agent. Unless that agent had gone AWOL on purpose. So many Hollywood movies depicted a disgruntled agent trying to leave and start a new life, only to be hunted and dragged back. Did that happen in real life too? Suddenly, I wanted more information. What if MI6 had done something underhanded, and this agent was doing the right thing?

The lift stopped and dinged. The doors opened, and we exited. Sunshine turned left without even checking any door numbers. He'd obviously been here before. Maybe they did a lot of dealings with criminals or informants at this place?

When we reached room 406, I dropped our no-notice spells and cut myself off from the power. Sunshine slid a gun from under his jacket. Oh, it was like that was it? The PIB sometimes used guns, but we mainly dealt in magic, so this surprised me. Every muscle tense, I was ready to draw power if need be, but I didn't open to the river yet, just in case there was a witch in there. They'd have no idea who I was, so I'd have the advantage.

Sunshine waved the keycard in front of the door, and it clicked open.

He immediately flung the door open and jumped into the room with his gun held out in front. He spun one way, then the other, the gun travelling in a semicircle. He motioned me inside, then hurried to what I assumed was the bedroom, then bathroom. I waited until he'd called "Clear!" before I shut the door.

As he walked back in, he slid his gun into the holster at his side. "I hope that didn't scare you." I figured he was trying to be nice, but it was also patronising. Meh, I needed to get over it. Who cared if he didn't know what I'd been through and assumed by looking at me that I was naïve and green. At least he was being considerate.

I smiled. "Nope. All good. I'll just get to work. It'll probably take ten minutes or so."

He shrugged. "Okay, fine."

Before starting, I drew magic and asked to see any hidden cameras. Two glowed—one from the coffee maker sitting on the kitchenette counter, the other from the good old pot plant on a stand near the balcony. You'd think they'd find a more original place. Right, so someone was watching. I'd have to make sure the cameras couldn't see my phone screen at any time.

Sunshine stood in one corner observing me. Argh, an audience. Great. I turned my back to him and whispered, "Show me the last time Agent Riverbed was here." Instead of taking photos, I videoed. Even if there was no movie to see, I could move around and get all angles more easily. The more I used my magic, the more stamina I had, so this wouldn't drain me.

The lights came on. The blinds were drawn, so I couldn't tell if it was day or night. A slim blonde woman in a figure-hugging red dress appeared in the middle of the room, a man with her. The man had dark hair, olive skin, and dark eyes, a small, white scar at the edge of one eyebrow. He was of Asian descent, maybe Chinese? His straight black hair was cut fairly short, the fringe hitting his eyebrows. He had a short-sleeved black shirt on, which showed off slim arms, one of them coloured red and black with a full-sleeve tattoo of a serpent-style dragon twining around it. Agent Riverbed was handing the man a foolscap-sized, bulging, yellow envelope. Right. Interesting.

I walked around them both and filmed, making sure to get all the details of what he looked like. It would be important for identifying him later. I pressed Stop and lowered my phone. Next, I would just take photos because I wasn't getting anything special, and I already had the details I needed.

Again, I turned my back to Sunshine. "Show me what's in the envelope."

Riverbed stood there, her arms folded. Her face lacked emotion, but her body language said she was worried or nervous. The man had the envelope open, and he held two large wads of cash bound with rubber bands. From what I could see inside the envelope, it was all cash. I took a close-up of the Euros. Maybe there would be some identifying numbers MI6 could look into… unless this was all a sting, and it was their money. I really knew nothing about what was going on… nor did I want to. My life was in enough danger as it was, and I appreciated that things were on a need-to-know basis.

I lowered my phone and sucked in a breath. What if I found something out today that put me in danger? God, I hoped Angelica was right to trust Phillip and Agent Prentice. What if we had another director debacle on our hands?

"Are you all right?" Sunshine stared at me, lines of worry stamped in his usually smooth forehead.

"Um, yeah. Sorry. Sometimes my thoughts run away from me." I forced a smile. "I'll be done in a few minutes." He gave me a curious look, probably wondering what the hell I was actually doing but disciplined enough not to ask. He likely assumed I wouldn't tell him anyway.

Again, I turned my back on him, and whispered, "Show me what else happened." I lifted my phone, but it was like a movie. Crap. I switched to video. The man smiled, and it was about as friendly as a rabid bear. Riverbed chuckled nervously and took a step back. She could read him too. He gave a nod, as if he were saying goodbye and went to the doorway, walking straight through me. I shuddered and hurried behind Riverbed's shoulder so I could film them both.

Once he reached the doorway, he turned and said something my magic didn't let me hear. He laughed and started shoving the envelope down the front of his jeans, then covered it with his shirt, but he'd done a sneaky and pulled out a gun with a silencer. Crap. He'd managed to get far enough away that her combat skills couldn't help her. He wasted no time firing two shots. One hit her middle, the other her chest. She stumbled backwards. He ran to her, put the gun to her temple, and fired.

I swallowed, my breath coming faster. Blood and brains everywhere, I was glad I couldn't hear the sickening thuds as her torso and head hit the ground. As soon as it was done, he stepped away and made a phone call.

Then he left.

Even though I wanted to throw up, I made sure to film the room, to show where they needed to look for evidence. When I stopped filming, I noticed the rug she'd fallen onto was different. The curtains were a slightly darker shade of brown. And, of course, her body was nowhere to be found.

I looked at Sunshine who was staring at me, still worried. "Um, can you do a quick check of the cupboards and under the bed? Make sure we haven't missed anything?" Surely if they'd left her body here, it would be smelling to high heaven.

Just so I didn't leave anything to chance, I grabbed a tea

towel from the kitchenette and opened the balcony door—no sense in contaminating the scene with my fingerprints. I stepped out. "Show me the outside at the time Riverbed was killed." It was as if God turned a big light off in the sky. City lights blinked into existence. So, night-time. I took a few photos of surrounding buildings and the illuminated complex pool, which was a pretty rectangle of aqua, the white poolside lounges occupied by only two people.

And that was that. I took a deep breath and went back in, locking the door behind me. Sunshine waited. "Are you almost done?"

"I'm done. Let's go." I didn't want to travel from here because if someone had noticed us coming into the building, they would wonder why we didn't come out again, and I didn't want to tamper with the surveillance because it wouldn't ring true to whoever was spying that they both just broke and all of a sudden, we disappeared out of the frame.

It was time to take all this back to Prentice. Not a moment I was looking forward to.

❧

Agent Prentice, silhouetted by the light coming through the windows at his back, sat in his chair and stared at his laptop screen. His jaw bunched from the tension of jamming his teeth together as he watched my footage… for the fourth time. Finally, he looked across his table at me. "This…" He rubbed the back of his neck. "I just…" I wasn't sure if he was referring to the fact that I pulled this back from the past or that someone he worked with was murdered, and he'd seen every gruesome detail. I didn't want to speak. I'd give him time to say what he wanted. Even an experienced agent might need processing time, especially as he probably hadn't expected what I was going to show him. Agent Sunshine had reported back here with me, then left straight away, which was a relief. I wasn't sure if they would really keep their promise about people finding out.

Prentice stared past me to the picture of Queen Elizabeth for a bit, then looked back at me. "I know this is real, but it's hard to believe you actually captured this." His heavy sigh settled over both of us, my heart feeling its burden of sadness. "She was a good agent. I'm not going to tell her family until we find the body. As far as they're concerned, she's missing." He glanced at his laptop screen again. After shaking his head for the millionth time, he looked at me. "Thank you for doing this, Agent Bianchi. Your talents are a miracle. I appreciate you sharing them with me. I know how dangerous it would be for you if this information got out." I didn't know what to say, so I just nodded. "By the same token, I need to ask you to stay mum about what you saw. You can't speak a word of this to anyone—not Agent DuPree, not any of your PIB agents."

"I know. As far as I'm concerned, nothing happened. I've deleted everything from my phone, as you've asked. You have the only copies of the information." I bit my lip and silently scolded myself. I needed a poker face stat. It wasn't in my nature to lie, unless of course I was protecting myself or a loved one, but if things got out of control and someone else ended up coming after me because of this, I wanted proof about why, and leads to chase up. I'd sent everything to my laptop at home. I would never show anyone, but it was my insurance policy, just in case. Also, Angelica might have warned me to do it for anything I filmed for them. "I can keep my mouth shut if you can." I gave him a sad smile.

He returned it. "It's my job to keep my mouth shut, Agent Bianchi. Your secrets are safe with me."

"Thanks." I wanted to ask more questions about the case —was she working for MI6 at the time, did he have any idea who that man was, why was she at the hotel alone without backup if she was working for them? But I couldn't. This wasn't a PIB case where Angelica valued my input…. Well, she valued it some of the time. Tentacles of regret and frustration tried to anchor me to the chair, but I stood, knowing the meeting was all but over. "Well, if you need me for anything else, just call."

He stood, held his hand out, and I shook it. "Thank you, Agent Bianchi. Your *help* has been invaluable. It's like nothing I've ever seen, and whilst I hardly believe it, it's going to make a big difference into whether we find Agent Riverbed or not."

"Do you mind if I leave from here?" It wasn't like anyone else was here. Besides, they had an exit room, so it wasn't as if most of the people who worked here weren't aware of travelling.

He put one hand on his hip and the other raked through his hair. "Ah, yes, sure. Have at it." He seemed nervous. Had he never seen anyone do this before? It wasn't like it was anywhere near as secret as my other talent he knew all about. Oh well, he was about to get an education.

I made my doorway, put the coordinates on it for Angelica's country-house reception room, and stepped through. It wasn't quite five, so no one was home. I wouldn't be surprised if I was by myself till six. Hmm, time for a bubble bath. It had been a crazy couple of days. Before I trundled upstairs, I stuck my head into the living room, hoping against hope that…. Yes! All the cages were empty. Woohoo! I grinned. An unexpected *nice* surprise for a change.

After my bath, I went downstairs to the reclaimed living room, curled up on the couch, and turned on the TV. Abby and Ted came in and sat with me while I watched the news. A segment came on about Australia. Wow, they were having a lot of flooding. So sad. It made me miss home. Where I used to live would be fine, but one of the places they'd named in Queensland was somewhere a friend of mine lived. I pulled out my phone and texted her. Oh, that's right, it would be super early in the morning for her. Argh, stupid time zones. Hopefully she'd get back to me later.

A yearning to return tore through me. The prickly heat of tears assaulted my eyes. Yes, most everyone I loved was here, but I had a few close friends still there; plus, it was where I'd grown up. All my memories and good times, the relaxed way of life, the fact I could grab a coffee and hang out at the beach with not a care in the world. Those days were gone. Maybe I mourned them just as much as Sydney.

Please, please, please, universe, can we get through all this drama and go to Sydney for our wedding?

Abby nudged my hand, demanding a pat. "Thanks, Abb." She knew when to pull me out of my spiralling. I should just celebrate today's win—we had our living room back. I changed the channel to what had quickly become my favourite game show—*Tipping Point*. Settling back, and with Abby purring, I made the most of my relaxing afternoon. I'd look at that info Angelica had given us this morning and memorise the baddies tomorrow.

I'd had enough negativity for one day.

CHAPTER 7

The next morning, I got up at seven so I could start reading through the info on the bad guys. I studied until ten and went into HQ to meet Imani in the grounds. She was going to help me train the squirrels, but with her standoffish vibes, I wasn't sure how the squirrels would take to her. They needed cajoling, and I wasn't sure if she was capable.

She was waiting for me when I exited the main doors. "Lily, morning, love. I missed you at breakfast this morning."

"Meh, I was studying up on those stupid criminals. So many ugly mugs, and I have more to get through this afternoon." I stopped next to her, and seven squirrels came running, GTB in the lead. He jumped onto one pants leg and scurried up to sit on my shoulder. "Well, good morning, cutie. How are you?" The four other squirrels waited patiently near my feet. Well, this was a good sign—they didn't look timid at all.

Imani chuckled. "Your fan club, Queen of the Rodents."

I made a stupid face. "It's better than being the queen of nothing… like you." I smirked.

She laughed and shook her head. "You're such an idiot."

"I know. And?"

GTB chittered. *You're not an idiot. We love you.*

"Aw, thanks, sweetie." I looked at Imani and raised a brow. "Did you hear that? They love me. So ner."

She rolled her eyes. "Yeah, yeah. Don't let it go to your head. Those tree ra—"

"Hey!" I scowled. "They can understand, you know. You're supposed to be helping me here."

Another eye roll. "Fine." She looked at GTB and smiled. "Good morning, Grey the Brave. How are you?"

Fine, thank you.

I didn't miss her small smile, as much as she tried to hide it. She cleared her throat and reinstated her serious look. "So, what are we doing today?"

"I thought we'd work on desensitising them, get them used to loud noises, voices, and to coming when we call them, even with other stuff going on." Because if we couldn't get them to operate in tricky situations, they'd be useless. At any random noise or movement, they'd scatter like that day in Angelica's Westerham backyard when Will came out the back door. What a disaster that was.

A couple of little clicks, and a picture popped into my head. *Nuts?*

I looked down at the squirrels near my feet. Ha, Dusty. What a surprise… not. I reached into my pocket and gave them each an almond. "Just one. When we've done some training, you can have another one." I needed some leverage. They did want to help, but I had a suspicion their desire for food was probably stronger than anything else. I knew their currency. "Here you go." I handed one to Grey the Brave. "I'm going to call the other squirrels now, so try not to run away." Imani smirked. She had absolutely no faith. Unfortunately, I couldn't blame her. "Team Turmoil, report for duty." I put my pointer finger and thumb between my lips and whistled loudly.

Grey fluffballs came bounding from everywhere. I laughed. Imani's eyes were wide. Too funny. The joy of it filled my heart. When they'd all reached us, I took a headcount. "Um, wow. We've gained some members." I looked at Imani. "We started with twenty-eight, and now we have thirty-five."

"Nice work, I think."

Grey the Brave chittered. *We've been recruiting some squirrels from around here. They're going to tell more too.*

"Thank you so much! We're going to build the best squirrel army ever." Okay, so it was the only squirrel army that ever existed, but still…. I held up my hand to him. "High-five me."

What?

"I'll show you." I looked at Imani and held my hand up. She stared at me, deadpan. "Give a sister some love. Don't leave me hanging."

She gave me a look that said "I can't believe I'm doing this" and raised her hand. I slapped it. "Like that." I put my hand up to him again, and he raised his little paw, and we touched palms. "Nice one!" I could feel his confusion in my mind. He was wondering why it was a thing. Oh well. I'd get them all on board eventually. "Okay, team. It's nice to see all of you. Do you know how to line up?" I imagined them standing in a long line and sent the thought to them. Tails and whiskers twitching, they scrambled around, eventually forming a long, snaking line. "Nice work! Now I can hand out a nut to everyone." Some would end up with their second, but they deserved it. I went along the line and gave each one a nut. GTB was still on my shoulder though. "Are you my second in charge now?"

Imani planted her hands on her hips. "Hey, love, what about me? I'm not going to be outranked by a tree r— um, squirrel."

I smirked. "Fine, you can be 2IC. Sorry, Grey, you'll have to be third in charge." I could tell him to get down there with the other squirrels, but his intelligence was superior from what I'd seen, and I could use his help wrangling his comrades. "Right. Now you've all had your nuts, we're going to work on not being surprised. I'd like you all to raise your paws if you understand." I sent them a mental image of a squirrel raising its front leg. I also raised my arm. "Like this." Some of them made little squeaks, and I had a feeling of understanding, but a few had their heads cocked to the side, and I was feeling confusion. "Grey, can you show them?"

He raised his "arm" in the air. I felt rather than heard a collective sigh of understanding, and one by one, each squirrel raised its arm until they all stood there with one paw in the air. "Excellent! Okay. Here's what we're going to do."

We spent the next couple of hours training, until I could see their attention and energy flagging. Work done, Imani and I left a whole lot of nuts for them with the promise to be back later in the day. I didn't want to overdo it with them, but we probably needed to reinforce what we'd just taught them later today and over the next couple of days so it stuck. If they were as scatterbrained as me, it couldn't hurt.

It was time to keep studying our enemies. Imani was happy with me doing that in her office, so we grabbed lunch and took it there. After an hour or so, I flipped another page. I sucked in a breath, and my heart raced. It couldn't be.

"What's up, Lily?" Imani sat opposite me in her plush office chair.

"Um, maybe nothing. This guy just looks familiar; that's all." I slid the booklet around on the table so it was right side up for her.

She pulled a non-committal face. "I've never seen him before. Maybe he just has a common face?"

"Maybe?" I pulled the booklet back to me. Hmm. I magicked my laptop from home, opened it, and searched up a certain file from this morning. Thank God I'd kept the footage. My laptop wasn't facing Imani, so she couldn't see what I was looking at. I brought up the photos from today and stopped on one that showed the man who'd killed Agent Riverbed. I put the paper next to the screen. Yep. That was him, unless he had a twin. There was no mistaking the little white scar intersecting the edge of his left eyebrow.

But could I say anything? I'd promised, well more than promised, not to say anything about what I'd done with MI6. Going against them would mean possible gaol time. This was for a good cause, but still. Rather than saying anything to the PIB, I should tell Agent Prentice about it, if he didn't already know. If this guy was on our radar, he was probably on theirs. But it wasn't great that he was fraternising with witches. This guy, from the info on my sheet, wasn't actually a witch but one of the criminal organisation's cronies.

What was he doing killing an MI6 agent? Had the directors put all the puzzle pieces together? Was this random or only the beginning of them killing agents from MI6. Payback maybe?

"I have to make a call." I closed the files and sent my computer back home. "Be back in five."

"Right you are, love." Imani looked up briefly before studying her booklet.

I slipped into the hallway and called Agent Prentice's mobile. "Agent Prentice speaking. How can I help you, Agent Bianchi?"

"Um, I was wondering if you already knew who that man was from this morning." I wasn't going to say anything over the phone, even though he probably had it secured with all the tech in the universe.

"We haven't gotten that far yet. Why?"

"I know who it is." He went quiet. Had I made a mistake? I didn't know how, but I still didn't trust him totally.

Finally, he answered, "Have you got five minutes to come in now?"

"Yes. See you soon." I hung up and returned to Imani's office. "I'm going out for a bit. Be back in about fifteen minutes."

She looked at me. "Ooh, cloak and dagger. What's going on?"

"I just have to do something. Sorry. I can't say."

"Ah, something to do with MI6." She smiled. "It's fine, Lily. See you when you get back. Be careful."

"Will do." I went to her outer office and made a doorway to MI6. After being cleared by the guard outside the door, I went straight to Prentice's office with my booklet. Angelica hadn't said anything about this stuff being classified. Not that I wanted Prentice to know what information we had. He still could be in with the directors somehow, but then, why would he call me in to investigate the murder of one of his agents if he knew. Was he setting me up to see what we knew? Argh! Damn. Well, Angelica had pimped me out to MI6, so I'd just have to take a leap of faith.

I stopped at his door, and before I went in, I took a deep breath. After a moment, I knocked.

"Come in." I went in and shut the door behind me. "Sit. So, what have you got for me?"

I dropped into one of the chairs in front of his desk. "I was looking through something for the PIB today. If you don't mind, just look at this page. The rest is confidential." There was no point telling him what that something was. At least I was still being kind of secretive. I held the booklet open at the page with the killer on it.

His blond eyebrows rose. "That's him." He read from the page, "Lingyan Chan, but he goes by Bobby Chan. Member of the Chinese mafia concentrated in Italy with branches here and all over Europe." He looked up at me. "So, what is he doing killing one of my agents?"

"I'm sure you can come to the same conclusions I can. Either it's a coincidence, or someone knows you're controlling the PIB now and they're doing what they can to sabotage both of us." If there was a third option, I had no idea what it could be.

"That sounds about right, and honestly, there aren't many coincidences in this job. Can I ask why the PIB is looking into him?"

I bit my lip. Argh, if Angelica trusted him enough to send me over here, and let them fund the PIB, surely I could trust him too. They were MI6 for goodness' sake. Also, didn't Phillip help Angelica, James, and Millicent track down the gang members? I was sure Angelica mentioned he was helping with some resources. Chances were, he was safe, and in the interests of helping that poor agent get justice, I might as well just tell him. "He's a member of one of the three criminal organisations working for the directors, which is why I suggested he's trying to sabotage you. I might speak to Ma'am, see if she can meet with you and give you more intel. I have a feeling you're going to lose more agents before this is done." I frowned. So much death, and all for money and power. It was disgusting.

Prentice looked as annoyed as I felt. "I'd appreciate that. Thank you. Could you possibly do that today? Also, I give you permission to tell Ma'am that this man murdered one of our agents. Don't give her a name though. I still have a lot to think through."

"Okay. Thanks for giving me some leeway. She'd probably need a reason to discuss this with you further anyway." There wasn't anything else to talk about, and I wasn't about to let him look through the rest of the booklet until I'd gotten the okay from Angelica. "Mind if I make another doorway here?"

He gestured to the middle of the room and gave a small smile. "Be my guest."

"Cheers."

As soon as I returned to the PIB, I went straight to Angelica's office. My mother was sitting in the outer office working. "Lily, sweetie, how are you?" She stood and gave me a hug.

"Hey, Mum. I'm good. How's it going here? Catching up?"

She blew out a loud breath. "With everything going on and Angelica not managing our normal cases, I'm fielding all the updates from Agent Link and sending on any urgent things that no one else can deal with. The others, I answer, or I delegate to your brother or Beren. I'll be happy when things go back to normal." I was proud of Mum, although maybe still a little frustrated. She'd settled into her changed role well, but I wished she would try and get her magic back. What if Beren with my help and linking to the power could help her? The problem was that a small grain of hope was better for her right now than trying and knowing that door was shut forever. And it wasn't up to me to push her. She was an adult, and I had no doubt that Angelica would prod her every now and then. I just hoped one day she'd be ready to try.

"Is Ma'am in?" I didn't want to show any disrespect or over-familiarity by calling her Angelica in front of other agents. To make sure I didn't slip up at HQ, I made sure I called her Ma'am even when there was only family around.

"She's in there with James. I'll just check if you can go in." She picked up the receiver of her office phone. "Hello. Yes. Lily's here. Can I send her in?" She waited a moment. "Okay. Bye." Mum looked at me and smiled. "Go in, sweetie. But she's only got five minutes."

"Not a prob." I knocked, then opened the door.

James turned around in his seat, and Angelica looked up from her laptop. "I didn't expect to see you this afternoon. What's up?" She never minced words, which was fine. No one had time to muck around.

I put the booklet on her table at the page with the Chinese guy. "The job I did today for MI6 was a missing-agent investigation. I photographed this guy killing the agent, but I didn't realise who he was until I was studying up on our enemies afterwards. Without giving him any information on our other targets, I've informed Agent Prentice who this is, just in case he wasn't aware, and he says he wasn't. He wants to meet with you. I think their need for security just increased. The directors probably realise they're helping us, and, unless it's a coincidence, their agents are in the line of fire as well."

Angelica and James shared a concerned look. "Well, this isn't ideal." Ha, Angelica, always the mistress of understatement. She moved her gaze to me again. "Well, unless he has another motive for this killing, it's likely related, but I'd like to feel him out, see what other reasons there could be."

James leaned back. "If you want to meet with him now, go ahead. I can finish this by myself. Honestly, I think this needs to be dealt with sooner rather than later."

"Thank you, Agent Bianchi." She stood, grabbed her mobile phone off the desk, and made a call. "Yes, Agent Prentice, it's Angelica DuPree. Agent Bianchi's just explained your situation. Are you free now?" She waited a moment. "Okay. I'll be there in five. Goodbye." She slid her phone into her inside jacket pocket. "Lily, please contact our inner circle and let them know there's a meeting at home tonight at six thirty. And finish studying up on our targets. We're moving on this tomorrow."

I ignored the nerves stampeding around in my stomach. "Will do."

Without saying goodbye, she made a doorway and left. I took my phone out and sent a group text, then sat next to James and did as I was told. Hopefully by the time we were done with this operation, we would all still be here, and every person in this booklet of evil would be in gaol or dead. Either way, it wouldn't be long until we had the answer.

CHAPTER 8

Will magicked enough seats for everyone in the living room of Angelica's country house, and we were all here—including Sarah and Lavender—waiting for Angelica to turn up. I looked at my phone. She was five minutes late. It was unusual for her to ever be late, but it was only five minutes, and she was juggling a lot. I sat in between Will and Liv. Liv turned to me. "How's the wedding planning going? You know I'm happy to help, right?"

Millicent, who was sitting in front of us, turned around. "Ooh, me too! Don't forget me."

I chuckled. "Don't worry—I won't. I actually haven't done much. I didn't see the point until we… um… deal with our current situation." I didn't want to tell her that any one of us could be killed in the next few weeks. She would know without my having to say it and make it more real.

"Well, when you're ready, let me know." Liv grinned. "It's going to be so awesome. Do you have any idea of the dress you want?"

I cocked my head to the side. "Something off the shoulder. I'd like crystals or something on a tight bodice that then falls gracefully to the floor in a satiny fabric. I don't want a long train. Ooh, and the cake is going to be chocolate with chocolate-fudge icing, served with cream or vanilla ice cream and strawberries."

Will chuckled. "So, you've decided on the dessert but not the actual food?"

"Pretty much. Yep." I grinned.

"It's about what I expected."

Liv leaned forward so she could pin her gaze on him. "If you're not happy with how things are going, why don't you do your share?"

He put his hands up. "Hey, I wasn't complaining. Just making a comment on the fact that I know my fiancée." He looked at me. "If you want help, you know you only have to ask."

I smiled. "I know. You've offered twice already, and like I said, I'm not ready to really plan it yet. Besides, I think I know what I want for most of it, so it's fine. Besides, it's not going to be complicated. Something simple, outdoors."

Angelica strode into the room. "Evening, everyone. Sorry to keep you waiting." Everyone stopped chatting, and Millicent turned back to face the front. "Right, let's get straight to it." She stood at the front of the room, poker face on. Her serious tone meant every impactful word was seared into my brain. "Tomorrow, we begin phase two of our operation—going after the criminal operations tied to the directors. We'll dismantle their groups piece by piece until every one of their members is in gaol or in a casket." She wasn't usually dramatic, and I had a feeling that those words were meant not only as a pep talk but as permission to do what needed to be done. No questions asked. Kill them if taking them in was too dangerous.

She gave everyone a minute to digest that, then continued, "Today, it was brought to my attention that the directors are also targeting MI6 agents. Two have gone missing in the last week, one has been confirmed murdered." Her gaze found me, and I was sure I didn't imagine her subtle nod. Her attention moved to Will, then Imani. "But for tomorrow, we won't be utilising their men and women. We'll keep this in-house—I fear the witches we're dealing with are too powerful and organised, and I don't want to be responsible for the safety of non-witches, no matter how much skill they have in espionage." Her magic tingled my scalp, and the TV screen on the wall behind her turned on, showing an aerial shot of a mansion and its surrounds, including two resort-style pools, two tennis courts, and a basketball court. Totally loaded. "This is the home of Enzo Cozzolino in Italy. It's more of a compound, really. A six-foot wall topped with barbed wire surrounds it, and there are magical protections on the place as well. This is the first group we're taking down because they're the most powerful. If we can deal with them, we can deal with the others." She waved her hand, and different pictures of the house slid across the screen. Front, back, sides, and a couple of interior shots.

Will cleared his throat. "I assume we'll pick off gang members that aren't in the house first? I don't like our chances of getting into that compound if they're expecting us."

"You assume correctly. Their members are in the first chapter of the booklet I gave you all, which makes up about half the booklet. They're known as the Cozzolino Family Witch Mafia. There are a handful of non-witches, but mostly, they're witches of varying skills and strengths. The top echelons of the group are extremely powerful, hence why they're the top crime family in Italy. They, of course, have no scruples and have bribed and magically coerced local law enforcement, so we won't get any help there. In fact, we may get some interference. So when we do what we need to, it's get in and get out ASAP."

"How long is all this going to take?" asked Imani.

Angelica shared a "look" with James before turning back to Imani. "I want to hit nests of them simultaneously if we can. The more we get at once, the better, but I think we might have to start by disappearing one or two at a time. If we can pick our moments with no witnesses, they'll suspect, but they won't know for sure what's happening. I'm hoping this will take a few days, but realistically, it might take a week or more, at least to wipe the main players off the table. After that, they'll be in disarray, and our job will be that much easier. There might even be stragglers we don't find for months, but as long as the most powerful of the family are dealt with now, we should be okay. When we shut down the directors, their supporters won't have to do their bidding. They can slink off quietly."

I put up my hand, and Angelica gave me a nod. "So, what's happening tomorrow? Are we going to Italy to take a few out?"

Lavender chuckled. "Smiting Queen, cool your jets. We want to arrest as many as we can." He looked at Angelica. "Am I right?"

"Yes, and no. I don't want any risks. If you can't slap the cuffs on them quickly, kill them. I don't want any scenes that show witch powers in public or that attract unwanted attention. Word will travel fast to Cozzolino himself."

Lavender's eyebrows rose. He wasn't used to Angelica

shoving the rules into the bin. Angelica's gaze shifted to me, and her look was… pensive. "Lily, tomorrow some of us are going to Italy to start the process, but I want you and Imani here. I have a special project for you. It involves your ten smartest squirrels. I'm going to need them to help us infiltrate Cozzolino's compound."

I swallowed the lump in my throat that appeared out of nowhere. Not my squirrels! What if they got hurt or killed. Oh, God. I knew I said I wanted a squirrel army, but I didn't think we'd use them this soon. "Um, I don't know if they'll be ready."

She cornered me with her unrelenting stare. "They have to be." Pain lanced behind my eyes. Ah, the joys of a stress headache. Then it hit me—she knew about this before she told me I could train my squirrels. She'd already decided what their first job would be, and like an idiot, I ran straight into that spiderweb. Crap.

Imani, who was sitting in front of me to my right, turned and gave me a sympathetic look. "We'll get it right, love, and give them the best chance we can. Okay?"

"Will the mafia use guns to shoot them… or us?" I needed details.

Angelica didn't hold back. "Yes, dear. Some of the witches weaker in the power, and those who aren't witches, will certainly shoot at us and them if they know why they're there. Unfortunately, grey squirrels aren't that common in Tuscany."

"Can they wear little bulletproof vests?"

To be fair, Angelica tried to hide her smile, but my suggestion was obviously just too ridiculous. "Well, dear, they could, but then it would be obvious that they're not wild squirrels, and we need them for the stealth part of things. Maybe once they're out, we can put little vests on them, in case they get caught in any crossfire."

"Well, I might have one with me at all times, and since I'm a big target, I'll need that squirrel to be wearing one."

Imani looked at me again. "Lily, Grey the Brave is our smartest squirrel. He'll definitely have to sneak in and help deactivate security cameras and let us know whereabouts on the property the mafia members are."

I took in a deep, shuddering breath. This wasn't going well. And there wasn't anything I could do about it, except what Imani said: prepare my squirrels so they stayed alive. I couldn't even protect them with a spell because the crims would see it if they looked with their other sight. Argh!

Angelica gave me a sympathetic look. "Lily, I'll have little vests magicked up, and any squirrels helping us after the stealth part can wear one. Okay?"

"Thanks." I knew my sullen face didn't look appreciative, but I kind of felt duped, but how could I blame Angelica? What did I think was going to happen when I asked for a squirrel army? Note to self—don't come up with any other bright ideas.

"Lily and Imani, this is what I want you to do with the squirrels." She explained the skills they'd need and what commands they needed to know. "Right, you two can go back to HQ and start work while I go through tomorrow's operational details with everyone else."

Imani and I stood. When we went to the family room to make our doorways, I couldn't help but notice that she wasn't her usual, upbeat self. "Sorry you got stuck with me and the squirrels. You'd rather be in the thick of it tomorrow, huh?"

She sighed. "Yeah, but it's okay, Lily. It sounds silly, but those squirrels are going to be a huge help getting us access to that compound. What we're doing matters… it's just not as exciting as I'd like." She gave me a wry smile.

"I'll see what I can do to make it more dangerous if you'd like. I'll give them some stones to throw, and we can use you for target practice." I grinned.

She chuckled. "Actually, love, you might have something there. I think we need to do some magic in front of them so they don't freak out when weird things happen. I also wonder if they can feel the power in the air, you know, because animals can sense earthquakes and bad weather coming."

"Hmm, I never thought to ask them if they could feel it. Although they were the first to notice a magical storm was coming when Angelica's house got attacked."

We both made our doorways and went through to HQ. Gus answered the reception-room door. "Miss Lily, Agent Jawara, how are you both?"

"Just wonderful." Her words could be construed sarcastically, but her smile and tone said she was telling the truth. Argh, now I felt guilty that she was roped into helping me. Or maybe I was just being paranoid.

"I'm fine, thanks." I shut the door.

"I heard you're training a squirrel army, Lily. Is that right?"

I smiled, despite the guilt and worry for my squirrels and the situation I'd managed to put them in. "Yes it is. I thought it would be awesome, but now I'm just worried about them. They're going to have to help us soon."

Gus tilted his head to the side. "It'll be okay, Miss Lily. Once, I was stressed because we had to leave our dog with neighbours when we went away, but I needn't have worried. When he wouldn't stop vomiting, they took him to the vet, and he was fine by the time we came back. They weren't even that upset about their carpet, oh, and the cushion he ripped up because he missed us." He rubbed his chin. "Oh, and he dug up her garden beds. Come to think of it, they won't mind him anymore."

Imani and I looked at each other. Her lips twitched, and I pressed mine together. Ah, Gus and his stories. "Um, thanks for that pep talk, Gus. I'll remember that next time I'm worried about them." This time I let my giggle have its way.

"Glad to help, Miss Lily. Have fun with your squirrels." He grinned.

"We will. Thanks. You have a great day."

"Thanks!"

Imani held in her laugh until the lift doors closed and we were travelling down. "Oh my goodness. He's hilarious." She looked at me. "And honestly, love, don't stress about me helping. I'm happy to. Sorry for my pity party before."

The lift doors opened, and we got out. "That's fine. I feel guilty though. If you don't want to do it, can you ask Ma'am to swap you with someone else?"

"No, seriously, it's fine. Besides, she has her reasons. My job isn't to ask why." She held up her hand for a fist bump. "We're good."

I bumped my fist into hers. "Thanks."

As we crossed the front foyer, Agent Amy Plover walked past. I smiled at her, and she gave me the dirtiest look known to man. Whoa! Imani didn't miss a thing. She turned to watch her walking away. "Wow, love, looks like you've made an impression."

"Hmm, yeah, you could say that. I have no idea what I did. It seems like me existing is all it took."

She chuckled. "Maybe you remind her of someone she hates?"

"Maybe? I would've thought she might hate witches, but

she doesn't look at everyone else like that. It might be because I'm not a real agent and she resents me being here and at MI6?"

We walked out into the sunshine. At least the weather was nice. "Hmm. You know what, love? That's idiotic. You're one of the strongest witches who ever lived. And for someone who's had little to no training, you sure do a good job. I heard you helped solve a murder for MI6 just this morning."

I raised my brows and stared at her. "No one's supposed to know."

She waved her hand dismissively. "Ma'am was so proud of you that she might have mentioned something to me and Will because we had a short meeting after she returned from MI6."

"Oh, wow. Okay. That's unexpected, but I'll take it." Whatever I'd inadvertently done to Agent Plover, that was her bad luck. If she wanted to hate me, she could go for it all she liked. My friends had my back, and I had my squirrels and my magic. I smiled. Yep, other than the price on my head, life was just grand.

As we reached one of the park chairs on the grounds, I whistled for Team Turmoil. The trees came alive, and grey balls of fur scampered down trunks and hurried to us. When the sea of bodies was in front of us, I said, "Line up in two lines, please. Make each line fairly equal." I also sent them a mental image. I'd quickly learned that you had to be specific because what was logical to us might be unheard of for a squirrel.

Within two minutes, they'd arranged themselves into two equal lines. Imani nodded slowly. "Impressive. Nice work, Team Turmoil." A wave of pride and happiness pinged back at us. I basked in the warmth for a moment.

"Okay, stand by for your nuts." I gave a nut to each

squirrel in one line and Imani did the other line. Once we were finished, it was time to get serious. I pulled my list from my pocket. Angelica had given us very specific instructions, which I'd taken note of. I looked at my squirrels. "Okay, team, we have some important training today and tomorrow. There's a big PIB operation coming up, and I'm going to have to choose some of you for it. The squirrels we feel are ready at the end of the two days will be chosen. Is everyone okay with that? If you're not okay with it, put up your paw." My brave little cuties. Not one paw went up. I blocked off my emotions though—if I let my worry or guilt come out now, I might scare them. They supposedly understood what they were getting into when I'd originally asked them. But did they really?

Argh, those thoughts weren't going to help. What I really needed to do was focus so we could beat our enemies once and for all.

I stood straighter and did my best to exude confidence. "Right, Team Turmoil, this is what I want you to do."

CHAPTER 9

The next morning, everyone, except Imani and me, left at seven. Concern at what they were doing had me getting up early as well. I went into the kitchen and magicked food into Ted and Abby's bowls, then magicked a cup of coffee and sat at the enormous table… by myself. Staring out at the garden was usually relaxing, but today, it couldn't calm my nerves. At least we'd have surprise on our side. They knew we'd come for them eventually—they had to assume—but at least we got to pick the day and time. I just hoped that was enough to start rounding them up.

But anything could happen.

Imani, already in her uniform, wandered in when I was halfway through my coffee. "Morning, love." She magicked herself a cup of tea and sat opposite me. "They'll be okay. They're the best we have." She gave me a reassuring smile, but until they were home safely, I wouldn't be convinced. Instead of arguing with her, though, I decided to change the subject.

"Ready for another day in squirrel land?"

She smiled. "They're coming along in leaps and bounds." She snorted. "Get it—leaps and bounds."

I laughed. "Oh my God, your jokes are getting worse than mine. You've been hanging around me too long."

"You could be right. But seriously, they're learning much quicker than I thought they would. With a bit of luck, we'll have them ready by the end of today. I honestly didn't think it was possible."

"Who knew the average squirrel was as smart as a dog?"

"I know. Shame they're way flightier, but still, they're trying really hard." She hugged her cup to her chest.

I finished my coffee. "Want to get started?" Sitting here stressing wasn't going to get me anywhere, and my squirrels needed training if I wanted them to succeed and make it home safely.

She drained her cup. "Yeah, sure."

We made our doorways and went to HQ, but when I got there, something felt *wrong*. I looked down. "Oh crap."

Imani stared at me and burst out laughing. "Oh my God, love. You've lost the plot."

I cocked my head to the side. "I think I lost it months ago. Keep up." She laughed while I magicked my pyjamas home and my uniform on. One of these days, I'd get the hang of it….

⚜

Lunchtime finally rolled around, and I knew this because I'd been checking the time on my phone every fifteen minutes, also my stomach may or may not have been grumbling loudly as I hadn't had breakfast. The squirrels were losing concentration… and I meant that sincerely. They had actually done everything we asked with only minor hiccups. At least I knew that if we used them for operations, we couldn't make them do stuff all day. We'd manage them in shifts.

GTB was on my shoulder, and Imani had collected her own admirer—Hamstring. We'd named him that because biting people on the hamstring appeared to be his favourite mode of attack. He was a small squirrel but super feisty. His personality definitely suited Imani. I smirked. "Looks like I've converted you. You're now one of us."

She glanced at the fluffball on her shoulder and made a mock-surprised face. "Oh, what's that? I've never seen it before."

"Ha ha, very funny. You love him, and you know it."

"I'll never admit to it." She turned her head and whispered to Hamstring, "Sorry, but I have a tough-woman reputation to uphold. We'll just keep it between us."

Hamstring squeaked in what sounded suspiciously like laughter. The vibes he sent our way confirmed it. Having a sense of humour was a sign of intelligence. I had no doubt this squirrel was smarter than many humans I'd met.

"Okay, guys, it's time to go. I'll fill up your bowls, and I'll be back to run through this stuff again later this afternoon. Go rest for a couple of hours." I magically filled up the four bowls on the park bench, and GTB scampered down my arm and joined his mates at the food. Hamstring did the same.

Imani watched them, fondness on her face. "Gah, they've hooked me, Lily." She looked at me. "And I blame you. You've ruined me."

I laughed. "Yay me!" My stomach gurgled loudly.

She smirked at my stomach. "Time for lunch it is."

We went to the cafeteria and grabbed a table. But as Imani turned to go to the counter, I couldn't ignore the Godzilla-sized squirrel in the room any longer. "Do you think they're okay? Why haven't we heard anything? Can we see if there are any new people in the cells?"

She turned back to me, poker face in place. I still didn't know if that was better or worse than seeing her real feelings. I knew everyone did it to keep me calm. It wasn't exactly patronising, but it was useless because I saw through it. "I think they're okay. If there was an emergency, someone would've contacted us for help. Besides, they were splitting up into five smaller groups and going to different places. They couldn't all have been ambushed." She must've seen my eyes bug out. "What I meant to say is that probably none of them have been. We haven't heard from them because they're either waiting for their opportunity, or they're busy. Honestly, love. They'll be fine. You keep forgetting that they're experienced agents and strong witches."

"Argh, I know. It's just...."

She gave me a kind smile. "I know. Come on, let's get some food."

I could hardly taste my spaghetti bolognaise because I was mindlessly eating while my brain overthought everything. Maybe I should've gotten the bread-and-butter pudding—it would've held my attention better. That's what you got for trying to be healthy.

I finished eating and put my cutlery on the plate. "I can't wait any more. I'm going to go and see Mum. She'll give me a heads-up, surely." Mum and Liv were liaising on this one as everyone's safe point of contact. The one positive was that no one had contacted Imani or me for help. That was the only thing stopping me breaking out into a full-blown panic.

She stood. "Stuff it. I can't wait either. Come on."

Huh? So, Miss Cool, Calm, and Collected was just as worried. If only I could hide it as well as her.

As we walked to the lift, my phone rang. My heart raced as I reached into my pocket and took it out. Crap. It was Agent Prentice. "Hello, Lily speaking." I couldn't bother pretending to be an agent. Meh, it was what it was.

"Agent Bianchi, I'm glad I caught you."

"Um, is everything okay?" What if Angelica had contacted him because something had happened to Beren or James, and she didn't want my mum or Olivia finding out? I swallowed.

"One of our agents has been murdered. A member of the public found him in a laneway behind her house in London."

"He had agent ID on him?" Wasn't the point of secret agents them being, well, secret?

"No. He had a business card on him for Sterling's Accountancy. We have a department that just deals with those calls. They answer the phone as if that's the company."

"Oh, that's a good idea."

"Anyway, Agent Bianchi, I didn't call to discuss that. I was hoping you could go to London and take some photos. I'll send Agent Plover with you. She can keep the public away while you do your thing." Argh, not her. Anyone but her.

"It sounds like a quiet laneway if someone managed to kill someone else during the day with no one noticing. I'm sure if you gave me the address, I could just go there myself."

"Sorry, no can do. I need her to canvass the residents. Plus, I promised Phillip and Ma'am that you'd be safe at all times. If she's nearby, I'd feel much better."

I wanted to tell him that I could smite people, cut them in half with accurately placed doorways, travel to toilets with a single step, and that Agent Plover would more likely be a liability because last time I checked, she looked like *she* wanted to kill me. But he wasn't going to budge if he'd promised people, and God forbid it got back to Angelica that I'd been difficult. I sighed. "Fine. Am I meeting Agent Plover at your HQ or mine?"

"She was at the PIB this morning, but she's been here for the past hour. If you come to my office, I can brief you both, and you can go from here. See you in…?"

I pouted at Imani, who'd been staring at me and listening to my side of the conversation. "Five minutes, I guess." Might as well get it over and done with.

"Thank you, Agent Bianchi. See you shortly." He hung up. "Spill."

"I have to go investigate something for MI6, but get this —Agent Shoot Dagger Eyes at Lily is coming with." I pouted when what I felt like doing was throwing myself on the floor and having a full-blown tantrum. "Can you please let me know what Mum and Liv say? Text me as soon as you know?"

She gave me a sympathetic smile. "Will do. Stay safe, and come back to my office when you're done."

"See ya." I waved as I made my way into the corridor. After one agent walked past, the space was empty, so I made my doorway and went to MI6. The guard opened the door for me. "Agent Bianchi to see Agent Prentice."

"Yes, Agent Bianchi. Please go straight up." He basically dismissed me by turning to shut the door and standing in front of it, staring straight ahead. Fine. These guards weren't nearly as friendly as Gus. Okay, so Gus's stories left a bit to be desired, but it was always nice to see his friendly face.

Dread weighed down my footsteps. I was not looking forward to hanging out with Agent Plover. Why did she hate me? Would she stare daggers at me the whole time, or would she ignore me? I was hoping for the latter, which also meant that I wouldn't have to make painful small talk.

I reached Agent Prentice's door and lifted my hand to knock.

"*Squeak.*"

I froze. Was I hearing things? After working with the squirrels for the past couple of days and having all that stress, maybe I was truly losing it.

Chittering came from the floor, and my pants leg moved. I looked down. "Oh, crap. Grey, what the hell are you doing here?"

You seemed worried all morning, so I've been following you around.

"You're such a sweetie, but you can't be here." I looked around. No one else was in the hallway. "If I make a doorway, can you go through it to HQ? I'll call Imani, and she can open the reception-room door for you."

He made some adamant clicking noises. *No. I'm coming with you. You want me to learn things. This is how I'll learn.*

Oh, double crap. I rubbed the middle of my forehead. My life was becoming ridiculous. Okay, so we were way past "becoming." I sighed and sent him an image of him sitting on my shoulder. He chittered excitedly and climbed up. I was really going to walk into the office of the top agent at MI6 with a squirrel on my shoulder. "If you wee on me, you're never getting on my shoulder again."

His mood was… offended. *I'm not a baby. I know not to do that. Seriously, what do you think I am?*

I pressed my lips together. *Don't answer that, Lily.* Instead of insulting GTB any further, I knocked on the door.

"Come in!"

I pretended everything was normal as I stepped inside and shut the door behind me. Unfortunately, Agents Prentice and

Plover couldn't do the same. Agent Plover gave me a look like "ew disgusting," and Prentice scrunched his forehead. "Is that a squirrel on your shoulder, Agent Bianchi?"

"Yes, sir." I wasn't going to elaborate. Maybe he'd just forget about it and move on.

"I'm afraid you can't go to the scene with a squirrel. There are other agents there gathering evidence."

"He's in training, sir. I'm supposed to take him everywhere with me."

Agent Plover rolled her eyes. She looked at Prentice. "With all due respect, sir, why is she even here? Isn't this something our own agents can deal with? I've heard around the PIB that she isn't even a proper agent. She's a consultant."

He fixed a steady gaze on her. "She has special skills we need, and I can assure you that she's a respected member of their team. I won't be questioned on this, Agent Plover. We pay you to follow orders, not challenge my authority. I'm letting this go right now because of your current... circumstances, but don't let it happen again."

Whoa, massive smackdown. Even though it was self-inflicted, she'd have another reason to hate me now. GTB could likely feel my stress because he patted my head and sent me an emotion that felt like a hug. *Thank you, Grey*. Hmm, was he now my emotional-support squirrel? I pressed my lips together to hold back my smile. Wouldn't it be wonderful if Plover thought I was laughing at her getting chewed out. Yeah, no thanks. Also, what were those circumstances? Just that they needed me, or was it something more personal?

Agent Plover looked down. "Yes, sir."

Prentice stared at me again. "This is the address." He handed me a piece of paper. "I want you to find out everything you can. While you're doing that, Agent Plover will canvas the residents. Make sure you return together." Thank goodness she had work to do that wasn't in my immediate space. At least I wouldn't have to ignore her the whole time, or protect myself from her deadly glares. He also handed me a lanyard with my ID on it. "This is so you can attend the crime scene. All our agents need one. Actually, you can keep it. It will give you access in the future."

I placed the lanyard over my head, careful not to get it caught on GTB. "Thanks. Also, is it okay if we travel by doorway?" I wasn't going to assume he'd be okay with it every time, and since he'd just had to assert his authority with Plover, I didn't want to touch a sore spot.

He huffed. "Yes, that's fine. This is urgent." I didn't want to rub it in, that travelling the witch way was bloody awesome, so I didn't.

I hadn't sat down. "I'm just going to check where the nearest landing spot is." I could've said toilet, but Plover might as well get a surprise. I smirked as I searched the streets on the magical world map that only I could see. There was a public toilet two blocks away. Nice. I looked at the back of Agent Plover's head. "Agent Plover, have you travelled by doorway before?"

She answered without looking at me. "Yes. From here to the PIB twice."

"Great. So you know you don't want to touch the edge of the doorway because it can dismember or kill you. It's probably better if you stand next to me while I make it." See, I was behaving. I could've accidentally on purpose chopped off a piece of her foot. But Angelica would probably be a bit put out if I did that, and the blood would stain Prentice's rug. *Bad, Lily*.

Plover huffed and stood. She gave me a dirty look before

standing next to me. I made the doorway and stuck the coordinates on it. "Okay, you go first. When you get there, just move out of the way quickly so I can come through."

She gave me a wary look, as if she didn't trust me. All I could say to that was, ha—you made your bed....

Agent Prentice watched us. "Well, hurry up. We haven't got all day."

Plover scowled at me as if this was all my fault, then stepped through. I waited a bit, then followed. I came out in another stinky toilet cubicle. Plover was just going through the door as I entered. I met her outside.

She stopped on the footpath outside it and folded her arms. "Well, that was gross. You did that on purpose." Wow, no "thank you for saving time."

"Did what on purpose?"

She narrowed her eyes. "Don't play stupid with me. Putting us into a toilet block."

"It's where many of our landing spots are. We can't just go anywhere we want. There has to be an anchor point our spell goes to. Kind of like how a train stops at the station... sort of. Anyway, I'd prefer not to argue the whole time we're together. Why don't we just get this done so we can go our separate ways?"

She grunted. I'd take that as a yes.

I put the address into my phone and started walking. Why hadn't Imani texted yet? Had something bad happened?

After five minutes of walking and worrying, we reached the street that led to the laneway. The mouth of the laneway was taped off, and a police officer stood guarding it. "This is it." My phone dinged, and I jumped, which made GTB squeak and dig his claws in so he didn't fall off. At least he didn't run away. "Sorry, mate." I quickly pulled up the messaging app. It was Imani! I held my breath as I opened it. *Angelica is back at HQ with James and two of the witch mafia. Everyone else is okay and waiting for the right moment to nab their crims.* I sent back a quick *Thank God* and clicked to my camera app.

Plover sneered. "Texting friends while you're on the job. So professional."

She was obviously trying to get an argument out of me. What she didn't realise was that I was stubborn, and she wasn't going to get what she wanted. I'd dealt with way worse than her. I smiled and shrugged. "At least I have friends."

Her mouth opened, but nothing came out. He he he. Rather than wait for her to figure out a response, I made my way to the laneway entrance. "I guess you'd better do what Agent Prentice asked you to. I'm going to do my job now."

She narrowed her eyes but thankfully kept her mouth shut. I watched her stalk off to the front of the terrace houses that backed onto the laneway. Good riddance.

I approached the officer on duty. "Hi. I'm Agent Bianchi. Agent Prentice sent me." I showed him my ID.

The officer stared at Grey the Brave on my shoulder, blinked, then shook his head. When I didn't say anything, he must've decided it was too weird to ask because he looked at a piece of paper on his clipboard. "Okay, yes, you're cleared to attend. Just step over the tape."

I smiled. "Thanks." A couple of markers were on the ground along with an orange cone. Three agents stood around. One was writing notes while the other two discussed something. I gave them a wave. "Agent Prentice sent me to take some photos. Do you mind if I just get to it?"

One of the agents, a man with short salt-and-pepper hair and a close-cropped beard looked at me and did a double take at the squirrel on my shoulder. When he recovered, he gave a nod. "Go for it. We've done a sweep already. You shouldn't interfere with any evidence." Kudos to these law-enforcement people—they knew how to keep their curiosity on the back-burner. I could never be that patient.

"Great. Thanks." I whispered to my squirrel, "Okay, Grey, let's get started. I'm going to take some photos. Do you want to stay on my shoulder or wait on the fence?" I nodded at the brick fence that formed the boundary at the back of two properties. "I'm going to be lifting my arms up a lot, and it might get annoying."

Fence, please.

I smiled and put him on the top of the fence. He sat and watched as I turned. The other agents were also peering at me, but they quickly looked away when I caught them. I supposed I was a curiosity. They'd never met me before, and I arrived with a squirrel on my shoulder. Now I was going to be taking photos with my phone. Yeah, I could see how that didn't scream MI6 superagent.

Anyway, it was time to work. I whispered, "Show me the MI6 agent being murdered today."

I steeled myself for graphic pictures. I should've asked how he died so that I'd have a warning, but then again, was knowing and anticipating worse than not knowing? At least there didn't seem to be a lot of blood spread around the laneway. There were a couple of dark stains on the ground, but that could be oil.

The agent was a dark-haired man, but I couldn't see his face because it was on the ground. One man knelt on his back, keeping him there while another stood next to him, a gun with silencer pointed at the back of his head. I took shots from different angles. Show me five seconds after. A hole was in the back of his head, and the man who'd been kneeling on him stood. I took more photos, making sure I got the murderers' faces and their tattoos—both of them wore short-sleeved T-shirts.

Hmm, there was something there that I hadn't noticed before.

The agent's arms were straight by his sides, yet no one held them there. A faint blue glow of magic that traced the length of his arms explained why. I focussed in and took a photo of the little symbol. Probably a smaller version of a freeze spell, or maybe it was a hold spell. So why was the guy kneeling on his back? Maybe their magic wasn't strong enough to totally freeze the guy? Witches didn't all have equal ability or knowledge. Maybe that's what it was? I'd have to ask Angelica later. Now that witches were embroiled in this for sure, the PIB could get involved properly. I'd also bet that these guys were on our list.

Also, why this alley? *Show me how the agent got here.* I knew he wasn't a witch. Well, I didn't *know*, know, but if he had been, he would've been wearing a return to sender or something and would've been harder to kill.

This time, the men were stepping out of a doorway, the agent first, being pushed by the guy who would later kneel on him. The agent's arms were tight by his sides, that faint blue glow visible. So, that answered that question. They would've had to set up this landing place before they brought him here, and if it was temporary, it would only last a day or two. Permanent ones were hard to maintain. The PIB only managed it because they had a special department that kept the power flowing to them every couple of days. I guessed it didn't matter anyway, since I had their faces, and it wasn't as if the doorway led back to anywhere.

I whispered, "Show me how the men left." One of them had made a doorway. So, there you had it. End of story.

I went to the fence. "Okay, buddy. Time to go." GTB hopped onto my shoulder, and I said goodbye to the agents in the alleyway. When I looked at them with my other sight, it was clear none were witches. Did they even believe in witches? I wasn't sure how many of the MI6 staff knew about us. Why hadn't they educated all their agents—they did have a reception room, after all, but it was on a lower floor that didn't seem to get much traffic. Whatever, there was also a policeman on site. I'd have to drag my new *friend* back to the toilet and leave from there. Oh, the joy.

I went to the street off the laneway. Before I made it to the main street and the house frontages, yelling came from the laneway. I stopped, and GTB made some clicking noises. *Danger, danger.*

Magic vibrated my scalp. Crap. "Wait here." I placed him on the ground, put up my return to sender, and ran.

The policeman guarding the alley mouth was staring, his mouth open. Unfortunately, like most English police, he didn't have a gun, so there wasn't much he could do. By the time I reached him, he'd grabbed his mobile phone and was calling it in.

The two witches I'd captured with my phone were back in the alley, facing the agents. The witches had magical shields, but no return to senders. One of them laughed.

The agents hadn't drawn guns because these witches obviously looked like no threats; however, the agents were in shock because they'd likely just seen them step through a doorway.

One of the witches smiled. "We're here to even the score." His magic built.

Double crap. I couldn't not do anything. Angelica was

going to have some mind wiping to do, at least for the police officer.

Thank goodness they hadn't expected to find a witch here. I smiled and cast two freeze spells. Not as dramatic or fun as smiting, but effective enough. Both men froze, one of them still smiling. Idiot.

The agents stared at the men, stared at me, stared at the men, then back at me. I should probably explain before those spells drained me. "Um, do you know much about witches?" Two of the agents at least looked like they believed, the other, however, started laughing. "Okay, that's fine. In any case, these guys are here to kill you." That stopped him laughing. "I'm about to make a… portal and take them to the PIB. I'll call Agent Prentice when I get there so he can debrief you. Okay? Also, don't tell anyone about this because they probably won't believe you anyway."

They all just stared. Wow, and they wanted us to integrate with MI6. We had a lot of work to do. I made an extra-big doorway around the men straight to the PIB reception room. Once they were there, I stepped through and buzzed. Gus answered. "Hey, Gus. I need witch help ASAP. Can you call Imani here urgently please?" Gus had a pair of handcuffs hanging from his hip. "Ooh, are those the magic-cutting-off ones?"

"They sure are."

"Can I have them, please? I have two criminals here, and I can't hold two freeze spells much longer." Oh no! I'd left GTB at the crime scene.

"Squeak, squeak." *I'm here.*

"Oh, thank goodness! You're a clever squirrel." I'd also left that stupid Amy Plover there too. Meh, she could find her own way back.

Gus handed me the cuffs and called Imani. I slid the cuffs on the one who'd shot the other agent. Half the drain on my power stopped. Phew! It was like the relief you felt when you finally put down super heavy shopping bags.

The man swore, both in Italian and English, then lunged at me. I jumped back. GTB, however, jumped on the guy's leg, raced up his body, and bit his neck. The man screamed, and Grey leapt off and hid behind me. I chuckled. "Good boy! Nice work!"

I stepped out of the reception room and shut the door. "Let's leave them in there by themselves where they can't do any damage."

"Good idea, Miss Lily." Gus looked down at GTB. "Nice work, little squirrel. You've got your mum's back."

Grey chittered away, so I translated for Gus. "He says it's his job and that that man deserved it for being so mean."

"Too right, little guy."

Imani came jogging down the corridor. "Lily, what happened?" she called out before reaching us.

I gave her the super quick version. "I need help getting them down to the cells. Also, can you cuff one of them? I'm still holding the freeze spell."

"Can do." She opened the door, glared at the unfrozen one, daring him to try something. He wisely stood where he was while she handcuffed his mate. I dropped the spell. Ah, sweet, sweet relief. She looked at me. "We got this. If they try anything, spell them to sleep. It's fine to let them just fall on the ground. We can drag them."

I wasn't sure if she meant it, or it was just to scare them. Either way, it was funny, so I laughed. The one who'd lunged at me gave me a look not dissimilar to the murderous one Agent Plover had given me this morning. Oops, that's right. I had to call Agent Prentice. "Cool. I can do that, but just hang on a sec. I have a couple of urgent calls to make." I didn't want the crims to hear, so I went out into the hallway. Angelica was my first phone call. I quickly explained what happened. "So, we need a mind wipe out there."

"Right, dear. Send me the address. I'll call Agent Prentice for you as well."

"Thanks. Just explain to him that the witches I caught are the ones I photographed killing his agent. I'll bring him the photos later. Oh, and can you get Agent Plover from the scene. I left her there in my hurry to bring the scumbags back."

"Not a problem, dear. Once they're locked up, text me and let me know who they are and if they're on our list. Meeting in the conference room when I return. I'll text you when I'm ready. Bring Agent Jawara with you."

"Okay, will do. Bye."

Imani and I took them down to the cells and locked them in together. More than half our cells were occupied, and it was only going to get worse before it got better. They'd even added extra beds, so cells that were only for one or two were now for four.

After we did that, I had to fill in a form describing what had happened. They refused to state their names, so we looked through the booklet. "Bingo!" Imani found them both. "Nice work, Lily. They weren't two of their strongest witches, but they're first cousins to Cozzolino himself."

I smiled. "Nice that *they* came to *us*. It'll save Angelica a trip." Grey the Brave, who was still on my shoulder, squeaked with laughter, which made me and Imani laugh.

"Having fun, I see."

I shot to my feet and turned. "Will!" I would've run and

thrown myself at him, but he was with Beren, and they had three men in handcuffs.

He grinned. "Let me put these guys away, and I'll come back. I've got some of that to do too." He looked at my paperwork, then back at me. "What are you doing down here anyway?"

Imani jumped in before I could. "She caught a couple of Cozzolino's cousins." Hmm, say that quickly three times. "All in a day's work, hey, Lily?"

Will's eyes widened, and Beren smiled. "That doesn't surprise me, Lily. Nice work. If you don't watch it, Will's going to get jealous that his fiancée's a better agent than him."

I laughed. "He'll get used to it eventually."

"I'm already used to it." He winked. My heart. He was the sweetest; even though we were all only joking, he managed to make it so that he wasn't joking. I knew he meant it. He was wrong, of course, but his support meant everything.

Beren chuckled. "Right answer, Will, my boy. Okay, let's get these losers into the cells. I've got better stuff to do than hang out with them all afternoon."

Once we were done, Imani and I went out to the squirrels, seeing as how we told them we'd be back. We ran through a couple of our drills and gave them more food. When we were ready to go, GTB tried to come with us. "I'm sorry, but you should stay here. This is where your family are."

But I want to come with you. He stared up at me with big, round eyes.

Oh. My. God. I was melting into a puddle with each second. Talk about cuteness overload. How could I say no? But was it a good idea for him to be around humans all the time and not his squirrel friends and family? "Um, I don't know if that's a good idea. What if some of the other squirrels get jealous or miss you?"

He blinked. *Jealous?*

"You know, when someone gets upset because they think someone else gets treated better or has better stuff." Hmm, squirrels didn't really have stuff. They lived in trees and ate whatever they could find. It's not like they sat there watching TV or wore the latest fashions.

He shook his head. *We don't have jealous. Squirrels don't care. They are happy when their family is happy.* I sighed. If only humans could be more like squirrels.

I looked at Imani. "What do you think? Is it a bad idea to bring him home?"

"It depends on whether you want a squirrel tagging along with you everywhere."

As much as I loved my squirrels, and Grey the Brave, I didn't want to have to worry about him everywhere I went. "You can come with me tonight, but only if you agree that I can't take you everywhere all the time. You need to live a squirrel life too, and I don't want to have to worry about you when I'm working."

He nodded. *Okay. I can accept that. So, I can come with you now?*

I smiled. He totally had my number. I was such a pushover. "Yes, you can come with me now." Angelica was going to roll her eyes, but it wouldn't be the first time, or the last.

My phone dinged. I looked at it. "It's Ma'am. We've got a meeting now in conference room one." As we made our way there, I realised how tired I was. I'd pretty much been on my feet all day, done quite a bit of magic, and had piles of stress on top of it all. What I wouldn't give for a bath, dinner, then bed, and it wasn't even five in the afternoon.

We arrived at the same time as Will and Beren. "There she

is. My squirrel whisperer." Will grabbed me and gave me a full-on kiss. He never did that at work.

"What was that for?"

"Just because I love you."

I narrowed my eyes. "Did something happen while you were off catching mafia members?"

"What makes you think that?" His innocent tone didn't put me off because I could see Beren's face. He forgot to go poker mode.

"We can talk about it later." I gave him another kiss. "I'm glad you're here and you're okay."

"Me too."

Beren pushed the door open, and Imani walked in. We all followed. Angelica was at the head of the table. Millicent sat to her right and James sat to her left. Next to him was a surprise… well, two surprises. Agents Prentice and Plover. Seeing Agent Plover made my neck and shoulders tense. Her expression was… moody. She glanced at me, then redirected her eyes to the table. Well, that was better than taking daggers all meeting. Unfortunately, it looked like we were going to talk about what happened this morning. Maybe we'd have to work more closely with MI6. It would be fine if Plover didn't work there. I'd once had a part-time job where I had to work with a girl who hated me. It got to the point where I'd feel sick before every shift. I eventually quit because facing evil glares and snarky comments all day eroded all happiness. But what would Angelica say if I asked not to work with Plover? Would she tell me to stop being childish and suck it up?

I sighed and sat next to Liv, and Will sat next to me, Imani on his other side. I hadn't told Will about Agent Plover's attitude, but Imani knew, and she threw me a sympathetic look. At least I had people on my side, way more than Plover.

Right. Time to do what Angelica would probably tell me to and suck it up. I had support coming out of my ears. I could handle a few dirty looks. GTB nuzzled my cheek as a reminder that he was here for me as well. I smiled.

"Right. We're all here. Time to get this meeting started." Angelica's magic tingled my scalp as she made a bubble of silence. Thankfully, her gaze slid over me and my squirrel. She was quick to adjust—I'd give her that. "The groups we're after are now targeting MI6 agents. Seems the word is out that we're operating under their umbrella. This gives us a new urgency since witches are targeting non-witch agents in the MI6—in other words, the majority of agents. Before we discuss this further, I'd like to confirm that MI6 is now going to be collaborating with us… or, rather, we'll be collaborating with them. I'll be assigning witch agents to help protect MI6 agents on the job. This situation is rather complicated, as you'll soon learn. Before Agent Prentice explains what's happened, I'd like to report that this morning's operations were a success. We picked up all the mafia members we were after, and Lily managed to bring in two more, both of whom were responsible for the murder of an MI6 agent this morning and almost murder of three more agents. We have a way to go, but good work so far, team." She looked at Agent Prentice. "Now, Agent Prentice will brief everyone on his news."

"Thank you, Agent DuPree." He kept his gaze on Angelica. "First, I'd like to thank you for bringing our agents home your quick way today." She gave him a nod, and his eyes moved to me. "Secondly, I'd like to thank you, Agent Bianchi. Today you solved yet another crime for us, and you saved four of my agents, rather than three. Agent Plover would've met the same fate as the three agents in the laneway, I have no doubt."

Everyone stared at me. I smiled shyly and ignored my hot cheeks. "Ah, I was there and got lucky. I had the element of surprise, and I used it well. I'm glad to help."

Millicent giggled. "Um, I think your squirrel has something to say."

"What?" I glanced at GTB. He had his little arms folded.

"I'm fairly sure he rolled his eyes when you said you got lucky." Millicent grinned. "Lily, there's no need to be modest. We've seen you in action. I'm just proud you didn't smite anyone."

"Hear, hear. I knew you'd get the hang of it eventually, dear." Angelica smirked.

"I did my best." I smiled.

"Well, whatever you did, Agent Bianchi, MI6 is eternally grateful. And that brings us to what's been going on. Our agency is under attack. We've had two agents go missing in the past week—one of them confirmed murdered, three attacked today, and two murdered today." Agent Plover's chin fell to her chest, and she stared forlornly at her lap—were the dead agents her friends? Also, I hadn't thought they had two missing agents or two murdered today. Looked like I wasn't helping with everything. Agent Prentice must've noticed my confused expression because I'd only been asked to attend one of the scenes. "Yes, Agent Bianchi, while you were dealing with that crime scene, one of our agents was poisoned at home. They ordered takeaway. The delivery person was masked and had sunglasses and a motorbike helmet on, so we can't identify them. We can't rule out that that one wasn't related, but coincidences are rare in our field of work, and we haven't had an agent murdered for a couple of years."

Will interjected, his expression sombre. "I'm sure Ma'am has already said this, but our sympathies are with you and your agents. We'll do everything we can to protect your people. I'm sorry witches are involved. It's why the PIB was created in the first place—witches have an advantage, and we can't allow them to use it for evil."

"Your words are appreciated, Agent Blakesley. I fear this whole situation has brought to light the fact that we need witches in our organisation on a daily basis. It would make what we do so much more efficient and productive. Part of the reason we held off is that witches using their… skills every day make it more likely the word will get out to the rest of the population, and Phillip has explained in detail why that mustn't happen—and I agree. The problem we have is that witches are now negatively impacting national security, and without your assistance, we can't hope to win and have a functioning agency into the future if we don't pivot and alter direction."

Angelica linked her hands on top of the table. "I'm sorry that your involvement with us has had a negative outcome. If we hadn't come to you for help—"

Agent Prentice put his hand up in a "stop" motion. "Please, you don't have to apologise. It's clear the PIB is necessary. Without it, the witch criminals of this world would have free rein. It's no good pretending witches don't exist. Sticking one's head in the sand doesn't make anything go away. It's time we dealt with that reality, I'm afraid. MI6 supporting the PIB was, quite frankly, long overdue."

Angelica gave him a regal nod. "Thank you, Agent Prentice."

"So," he continued, "what we have now is a precarious situation. We need your help to keep our agents safe, and I know you don't have nearly the number of agents we have, so one-on-one protection is out of the question. My agents are in danger on and off the job. And therein lies the problem."

Argh, this was a huge mess. How were we supposed to protect them 24/7 *and* take down these organisations? We definitely didn't have the manpower.

He looked at Angelica. "I'll let Agent DuPree take it from here."

"Thank you. So, team, you see the situation we're in."

And all because of those scumbag directors. The enormity of chaos they'd created was something we might not be able to overcome. And now it wasn't just the PIB at risk. MI6, England, Europe… where did it end? The criminal witches of the world were ready to take over. Everything would change if that happened. *Everything.* I took a deep breath and stroked GTB to calm myself before I spontaneously combusted with the stressful magnitude of it.

"We have, of course, come up with a plan. I'm pulling some of our agents off the day-to-day cases that can wait. Those agents will be redeployed to MI6 to accompany their agents on cases. For the rest, Agent DuPree Junior"—she gave a nod to Beren—"and Millicent's father are working on a wearable device that can detect magic use up to a range of a hundred feet. The device should be ready tomorrow. We witches can detect magic use, so we've never needed to invent one before. In any case, every non-witch agent at MI6 will be provided with one. Every employee of MI6 will receive a crash course on witches in the coming days, and they'll have to swear a magical oath." Wow, things were getting serious. "Once that's done, we can give them all their devices. If those devices detect magic, we'll deploy a witch agent to make sure everything is fine." She took a sip of water. "Unfortunately, the MI6 agents are going to have to stop ordering takeout and engaging in other risky behaviour such as leaving the house if it's not for work or necessities. Hopefully that will only be for a short while because, in two days, we're going for the Cozzolino compound. Now we've started, we need to act quickly because with every hour we give them, they're more prepared." Angelica gave us a few more minor details, and then that was it. "Dismissed."

In two days, my squirrels were going to be in the firing line. I bit my thumbnail. If there was anything I could do to keep them extra safe, I needed to come up with it before then. I blew out a big breath and stood. Will stood and turned to me. "I'm having a meeting with James about a couple of assignments we have tomorrow. I'll see you at home for dinner, about six thirty?"

"Okay." He and James left. I turned to Imani to ask if she wanted any help, but she was across the room talking to Beren. Instead, Agent Plover stood there. She looked at me. Just what I needed—some afternoon angst.

"Agent Bianchi, I'd like to apologise." Her words were quiet, as if she didn't want anyone to overhear. I glanced at Prentice, who wasn't even paying attention. If he'd put her up to this, surely he'd be watching to make sure she did it.

"Oh, what for?" Not that I wanted to make her work for it, but maybe she was only going to apologise for something small and not the whole shebang. I needed to know how to be around her. Did I need to keep my guard up or not?

"I'm sorry for being rude and assuming you didn't deserve to be an agent. I heard before I worked with you that you were the sister of Agent Bianchi's second in charge and fiancée to another agent. I thought you were a liability. I was wrong, and I'm sorry. I want to thank you for what you did today. You stepped up and saved us, and I want to thank you for…." She swallowed, and her eyes took on a glassy, pre-cry look. "My… my girlfriend went missing. Agent Prentice told me that based on your special investigation that she's d-dead." A tear rolled down her cheek. "Thank you for finding out. Now we just need to find her body and bring her h-home."

Oh, crap. That was horrible. That was her girlfriend? No wonder she'd been in a bad mood in general—her girlfriend had been missing all week. "I'm so sorry." I would've hugged her, but our armistice was new, and she might hate being touched. She seemed the type not to want hugs from strangers. "Um, I know we're not exactly best friends, and I don't really know you, but if you need anything, let me know. I can't imagine how horrible things are for you right now."

She blinked away her tears and stood tall. A glint of hardness shone in her eyes. "I'd be most grateful if you helped us find her body and avenge her murder. That's all I really want."

I pictured her girlfriend as I'd seen her, being shot, then dead on the floor. She didn't deserve that. The directors had so much to answer for, and it was time to make them pay. "I promise I'll do whatever I can to make those things happen." It was a good thing that keeping promises was my forte.

"Thank you." She held out her hand for me to shake. Her eyes radiated an earnestness I'd never seen in her. "Truce?"

I smiled and shook. Maybe we were going to get along after all. "Truce."

CHAPTER 10

The next morning, we all had breakfast together at Angelica's country house. Afterwards, Mum and Liv went to headquarters to do their usual, and all the agents, except for Imani, Angelica, and me, went back out into the wild to bring in more mafia bad guys. GTB had managed to finagle his way home with me last night. I can't say I minded, and Abby and Ted were happy to see him, but now we were back, and Imani and I took him outside for a session with the top twelve squirrels we thought could do what Angelica had asked of them. We only needed ten, but it was good to have backups in case something happened—one of them might decide they didn't want to go, or one of them might freak out when we got there.

We'd spent a couple of hours running drills with a fake house that Imani, two other agents, and I had magicked out of lightweight blocks. It had doors, windows, drainpipes, and terracotta tiles and was meant to simulate conditions they'd find at the mafia compound. Now the squirrels had an expectation of what we'd ask them to do, what tools they'd be using, and how they were meant to do things.

When we were finishing up, my phone rang. My mouth dried. "Hello, Ma'am. Is everything okay?" She didn't normally call for no reason. I was always on high alert when I saw her name on my screen and the people I loved were in the field.

"Yes, dear. Can you and Imani come to my office, please? I have an assignment for you. Please leave the squirrels there. *All of them.*"

"Yes, Ma'am. Bye." I looked at Imani. "We've been summoned for an assignment." Before Grey could say anything, I looked down at him. "I'm sorry, buddy, but I'm under instructions to leave you here for now. I'll come see you later. Okay?"

He nodded solemnly. *Okay. Be careful, Lily.*

"I will. Promise." I gave him a nut and a pat and made my way with Imani to Angelica's office. Not that I wanted to put my life on the line, but I was happy to take some of the load off everyone else. The more I did, the less they'd have to do, and the less I'd have to worry for their safety. Also, the quicker this crap could be dealt with.

I opened the door and went into the outer office. "Hi, Mum."

"Hi, sweetie. Be careful."

I blinked. "I haven't even gotten my instructions yet."

Mum's smile fell. "I know she's going to ask you to go out there and catch some of those scumbags. I worry. I am your mother, after all. It's my job to worry. Just be careful."

"I will." I went over and gave her a kiss on the cheek. If I stressed about James, she would stress twenty times more because she was our mother. It couldn't be easy for her, missing out on being there.

"Have to go now. I've got intel coming in." She put her hand to her headphones and listened.

Imani waved at Mum as I knocked and opened Angelica's door. "Come in and sit down, ladies." We did as we were told. "Right, this one is for you ladies because our target works at a women-only day spa in Positano. We have a landing spot organised on a boat at the dock."

"That's different." I'd never heard of making one on a boat.

"We have to be inventive on occasion." She slid a photo to us. Imani picked it up, and we both looked at it. "That's your mark—Tina Miglore. She owns and manages the place. She's a witch and the sister of Cozzolino's second in charge. There will be a mafia member or two watching the building. They're all on alert, which is why we need you ladies. I had an Italian friend of mine ring up and make an appointment. You're best friends celebrating Lily's birthday. You've bought facials for you to have at the same time, generous friend that you are, Agent Jawara."

She grinned. "I'm the best friend a gal can have."

"Are we using our real names? Won't they know them? And what about our faces?" If we had a list of them, they surely had a list of us—there weren't nearly as many of us. And since there was a price on my head, I was sure they'd all taken the time to check what I looked like.

"These will help." Her magic prickled the back of my neck, and a duffel bag appeared on her desk. She stood and unzipped it, proceeding to put a whole heap of things on the table. "Here are your wigs, holiday outfits, huge sunglasses, and Lily, you get a fake nose."

"Oh my God, it's… big and hooked. I'm going to look like Gonzo from *The Muppets*."

Angelica smirked. "Don't overstate things, dear. You won't be blue. No one will mistake you for Gonzo."

I gave her a deadpan stare. "Right. Great, then."

Imani laughed. "Look, Lily, it's fine. It's not like Will will see you. Besides, would you rather have a huge honker or be a target from the moment we step onto Positano's pebbly shore?"

I sighed. "This nose will be a target for every plastic surgeon on holidays there. I bet I'll have ten business cards by the time we get off the beach."

"Okay, enough faffing about. You have twenty minutes to change and step through your doorways. And please, for the love of scones and clotted cream, don't kill her. She's helped distribute drugs, which is enough for us to arrest her, but she's never killed any of our agents or anyone that we know of. She's more a target so we can rile up her brother. Apparently, she's good at calming him down when he loses the plot. The more agitated we can make them, the more likely they are to make mistakes." Angelica grabbed a sky-blue beachy-looking dress and Crocs and handed them to me.

My mouth dropped open. "That dress is fine, but I'm not wearing the Crocs. They're disgusting." She raised her brows as if to say don't argue. "Seriously, I'm not wearing those. Don't you have some thongs? I have a pair of nice sandals I can magic from home."

Her eyes widened. "Thongs? You're going to wear underwear on your feet?"

I scrunched my forehead. "No, thongs… flip-flops." I rolled my eyes. "Seriously?"

Understanding cascaded over her face. "Ah, yes, flip-flops,

of course." She waved her hand in a dismissive motion. "In any case, you're no fun, Lily." Angelica threw the Crocs in the air, and they disappeared, hopefully to a rubbish tip somewhere nowhere near here.

"Thank you." I magicked my dress on, then grabbed the oversize sunglasses and wide-brimmed straw hat. Before I donned my hat, I glued on the huge Roman nose.

Angelica magicked some thick make-up onto my face to blend the nose's rubber edges into my face. When she was done, she stepped back and stared at me. "Perfect! It looks real."

Imani snorted. "Real ugly. Ha ha."

I looked down at the Crocs she'd happily put on her feet. "My nose will never be as ugly as those"—I made air quotes—"shoes." I followed that up by pretending to stick my fingers down my throat and vomit. "I'll never be able to respect you again, Imani. I'm so disappointed right now."

I magicked my sandals onto my feet, slid the sunnies on, and plonked the straw hat atop my head. I snatched the bright-orange canvas beach bag from the table and slung it over my shoulder. "There. How do I look?"

"Not like you, which is perfect." Angelica smiled. "Okay, ladies, good luck. I expect you'll be back here in an hour with our latest cell occupant. Oh, and don't forget these. I think it's time you had your own pair now, Agent Bianchi." She reached into her drawer and pulled out a pair of magic-blocking handcuffs.

Yes, I'd tried to avoid becoming an agent, but it appeared as though I'd been sucked into it like a black hole—there was no getting away from it. As much as I didn't really want this as a job, I sniffled at the compliment Angelica had bestowed on me. Pride expanded my heart to overflowing, and I smiled.

"Thank you. This means a lot." I wasn't going to remind her that I really just wanted to be a creative photographer—she knew. This was me accepting her compliment and respect. I would never throw that in her face. Instead, I threw the handcuffs in my bag.

"Ready, love?" Imani's dark skin stood out gorgeously against her yellow sleeveless, button-down cotton dress. She rocked her black, pointy sunglasses. Unfortunately, the Crocs ruined the whole look.

"I am. Are you sure you won't reconsider those Crocs?"

She lifted her chin. "Never! I can wear the hell out of anything. Crocs can't bring my level of hotness down. Trust me." She laughed.

"Bye, ladies." Ha, Angelica was always there to "tactfully" tell us what to do. "Here are the coordinates."

They appeared in my brain. "Bye." I put them on my doorway and stepped through to a subtly unsteady floor in a cabin. The scent of brine with an underlying, unpleasant waft of diesel hit me. I could never live on a boat. The motion plus the diesel smell would have me throwing up 24/7. Plus, there were no squirrels out here.

The cabin door was open, so I went through it. "Hello, anyone here?" I expected there would be an agent minding the thing.

"Hello." A blonde woman dressed in a white captain's uniform who didn't look that much older than me met me in the lounge area of the boat. It was rather large with a curved, white leather couch and dining table with six chairs, but it looked about twenty years old. It had seen better days, but it probably still cost a couple of hundred thousand pounds. It was expensive to live large. "You must be Linda." She winked.

I grinned. "Yes, I'm *Linda*. Lovely to meet you." I was about to ask her name when Imani joined us.

"Anita! Long time no see. How have you been?"

"Imani!" They fist bumped. "I've been on leave. Mum was sick. I looked after her for a couple of months." Her face crumpled. "She passed of cancer three weeks ago. This is my second day back."

"Oh, love, I'm so sorry. Are you okay to be back at work?"

She gave a sad smile, the one you put on when things were crap but you had to soldier on. "Yeah, it keeps my mind off it. I was just moping around watching *Stranger Things* and drinking tequila. It wasn't pretty."

"Well, I'm glad to have you back. We'll catch up later, yeah?"

"Sounds good. Good luck, you two."

"Thanks." I smiled and quickly made my way up the few stairs to the deck. The boat was tied to a dock, which made for an inelegant but safe disembarkation. At the end of the dock, a portable timber walkway led to the town. Steep cliffs rose from the beach, buildings clinging to them like limpets overlooking the blue-green Mediterranean. I glanced at Imani's ugly shoes. "Good luck walking in those sweat factories."

"They're quite comfortable, actually."

I gestured to the crowd of people strolling the sandy beach. "Look around. No one's wearing them. You're the least stylish person on this beach."

She stared at my face. "And you have the biggest nose, Gonzo. Can we go now? We're going to be late."

"Sure. I hope they let us in for our facials. They might make you take your shoes off because it'll crash the vibe of the place." I snorted as I started up the stairs. It was a lot warmer here, and I was happy I was dressed appropriately, although it was hot and itchy under the prosthetic and make-up. Hopefully Angelica had used waterproof make-up because I was sweating up a storm already.

Imani checked her phone. "We should get there in about five minutes. Just keep going."

To keep my apprehension at bay, I took in our surroundings. The rendered and stone buildings, some painted bright colours, some not, all with the charm of old Italy, claimed my attention. We passed a couple of hotels. "Wouldn't mind coming here to stay one day. It's stunning."

"It is gorgeous, except for all the tourists." Imani chuckled.

"And the stairs. Maybe we could set up a landing spot on the beach and one at our hotel and just step between the two."

She laughed. "If only."

I cocked my head to the side. "If people knew about witches, it could all go wrong, but it could go right. I bet everyone here would pay to use our doorways so they could avoid stairs."

"Hmm, you could be onto something. Why don't you bring that up with Angelica next time we're in a meeting?" Her face was all innocence.

"I'll be sure to. I'll tell her you encouraged me to bring it up during work time as well. She'll be proud of both of us." I wiped sweat off my brow. "I need a swim and a drink of water."

"We're almost there." She nodded up the hill. "See that red building just ahead? That's it."

"Do we need a word for go? You can call it, by the way. Maybe you should detain her, and I'll do the handcuffs and the doorway."

"Squirrels is our go word." She grinned.

"Ha! I knew my squirrels were growing on you."

She gave me a mock pfft look. "Meh, I can take them or leave them."

"Oh, okay. Should I get Angelica to put you on a different project, then?"

She rolled her eyes. "Fine, I'll admit they're growing on me."

"Knew it!" Gah, why was it so hot? Sweat dribbled down the sides of my face. "Can we ask for an ice water before we get to work?"

She laughed. "Actually, that's a good idea. Distract her, then boom!" She glanced at me. "Well, not literally 'boom.' You're not allowed to kill anyone. Don't forget that."

"Yeah, yeah, spoiling all my fun." I rolled my eyes in mock disappointment. For one minute, though, I imagined we were here on holidays and were about to enjoy a facial. What would that be like, to relax and be a tourist, dining out, swimming, shopping? If we didn't make it through this and get our trip back to Australia, I was going to be monumentally annoyed. Okay, I'd probably be dead and unable to be annoyed, but why let that get in the way of my disappointment?

"We're here."

I stopped and looked at the place. A rendered three-storey building on the low side of the street. It overlooked the sea. The white front door had red-and-gold writing. Miglore Spa. "Looks nice." I made an effort to relax so I didn't seem suspicious. The problem was that we had our magic shut down, so no one could tell we were witches. It meant that if someone did happen to recognise me, I'd be at a disadvantage. I had no return to sender or shield. It was like walking down the street naked.

I pushed the door open and resisted the urge to magic up. A bell tinkled, announcing our arrival. The interior of the shop was cool and air-conditioned. I sighed in relief. The entry room had a slightly sloping timber floor, white walls, and colourful paintings of Positano on the walls. A counter with a receptionist was against the wall to the left. "Ciao," the middle-aged lady greeted us. It wasn't Tina. This woman had short, styled, greying hair. Her skin was as smooth as a twenty-year-old's, and just the way she stood hinted at grace. Italian women were next level. I felt like a potato next to her.

"Ciao." I smiled. "We have an appointment for two facials. Under the name of…" Ah, crap. Imani hadn't told me if she was using a fake name. "…Linda?"

"Oh, no, love. I put it under my name." She looked at the woman. "It's under Jalissa."

"Just one moment." Her Italian accent made the words sound sexy. While she looked in the book, the bell rang.

A larger woman who looked to be in her fifties exploded through the doorway—well, not literally. She pushed the door shut. Her cheeks and neck were bright red under her baseball cap. She took her hat off and fanned her face with it. "Woo-wee, is it hot out there! It's as bad a Texas summer." Her strong American accent bounced off the walls. So friendly, but so loud.

Imani and I smiled at her. The spa lady gave her a grimace. "I'll be with you in a moment." She looked back at me. "Please, come this way."

The complication level just tripled. There was always a chance someone else would be here other than Tina. It meant we had to be extra secretive and quick when we pulled the pin on the arrest. I hoped the receptionist wasn't a witch. It sucked to have no idea.

The woman led us down one flight of steps into a hallway, then into a door on the left. The room also had timber floors and a large picture window with an incredible view of the sparkling sea. Two reclining chair-bed things sat in the middle of the room. A set of drawers sat to one side, a whole lot of products neatly arranged on top of it. A gorgeous woman in a white lab coat, her dark hair arranged in an elegant chignon, turned from the drawers and smiled. "Welcome. I'm Tina. Please, have a seat." She indicated the two recliners.

We introduced ourselves and sat as the receptionist left, shutting the door after herself. Okay, well, this was a good start. Magic tingled my scalp, and I heard the faintest click. Even though my magic was locked up tight, my natural witch abilities were still functioning. I wasn't sure if Imani could sense the magic, so I gave her a pointed look, making sure Tina couldn't see. Had they just locked us in? Did they suspect something, or was that normal practice?

"Would you like a drink, ladies? We have an aperitif or, if you prefer, sparkling water."

"Can I have some still water?" Why sparkling water tasted different, I didn't know, but I hated it. Did bubbles have flavour?

"Of course." She looked at Imani. "And you?"

"Mmm, an aperitif would be nice. Grazie."

"Prego." Tina seemed nice. I hoped I wouldn't have to kill her. It was weird. I didn't expect drug pushers to be so put together and, well, nice. Not that five minutes with someone made you an expert on their personality.

Tina went to a bar fridge located at the back of the room. When she bent to open the door, Imani said, "Squirrels."

Oh, crap. It was go time.

I unlocked the portal to the river and drew all the magic I could hold. I threw up a return to sender and a shield and grabbed the handcuffs while Imani drew her magic and stood.

I tried to jump out of my chair, but it was semi-reclined, and I had to pull myself out like a beached whale. 007, I was not.

Tina spun around, a bottle of Campari in her hand. She had a shield up. Dammit! Imani and I glanced at each other. At least there was no return to sender. She probably didn't know about those. "Who are you? What are you doing?" She held the bottle up threateningly. Was she playing dumb?

"We're from the PIB, Tina. We're here to arrest you for your part in the Cozzolino mafia drug ring."

The door handle turned. I spelled it shut. The last thing we needed was for the receptionist to get involved. Magic pushed back on my spell, and someone pounded on the door. "Apri la porta!" A man's voice. The mafia had arrived.

"I don't know what you're talking about." The woman was going to try and lie her way out of it?

"Right, so we might as well just go home now." I rolled my eyes. "You can't be serious. You don't think we do a crap ton of research before we try and arrest someone? Save your bs."

The man bashed the door again, and there was another push against my magic. My forehead was sweating again because of the energy I was using to deflect it. Tina glanced at the door. She said something in Italian, but I understood a few words: *ufficio investigativo paranormale*.

Another magic joined with the first in trying to break through the door. *Crap.*

"We need to hurry this up. I can't hold the door much longer. There's two of them out there now." I held up my handcuffs. There wasn't much Tina could do to us with all our protections. Imani had about four inches on the woman, too, and a hell of a lot of muscles.

"Okay, *Linda*. Get ready." Imani advanced on Tina, who

waved the bottle as if she were going to smash her with it. The shield should take care of it. Surely the woman knew that?

"Just hold her down, and I'll get the cuffs on."

"Roger that."

Tina lunged at her with the bottle held out in front. Imani grabbed it and pulled, unbalancing Tina, who stumbled forward. She fell hard on her hands and knees. Imani threw the bottle to me and dropped onto her, forcing her onto her stomach. The woman grunted and snarled. Her mouth was open, her head thrashing as if she was going to get a chance to bite Imani.

Not happening.

I put the bottle on the floor and knelt to put the cuffs on her. I got them on one wrist, and Imani carefully moved while still kneeling on her so she couldn't get up. She pulled her arm around for me to click the other one on. Done.

"Tina! Tina!" More power coming from outside.

"We need to hurry." I stood and made my doorway, chopping the corner off one of the chairs in my haste. Imani dragged the woman to her feet. She kept struggling.

"You might want to be careful your arm doesn't get chopped off, Tina." It was fair to warn her. If she didn't listen, that wasn't my fault.

Imani shoved her towards the doorway. Thankfully, the woman stopped resisting.

"Bruno, Ciao. Ti voglio bene."

Imani pushed her through the doorway, and that was that.

Should I try and get rid of the other two? What if they were crims we were looking for? I stared at the door as the magic pulsed. I could pretend I wasn't there, drop my magic and hide behind the door, then build a doorway around them when they walked in. Could it really be that easy? Or was I really that stupid?

Damn it. If I stuffed up, no one would forgive me, and I could jeopardise everything everyone had worked so hard for. Reluctantly, I stepped through my doorway and dropped my magic. I hated leaving crap undone because it always came back to bite you in the bum. Guaranteed.

CHAPTER 11

Gus already had the reception-room door open when I came through. Imani stood behind our captive. She stared at me over the woman's shoulder. "What took you so long?"

"I'll tell you later."

She narrowed her eyes. "Okay. Come on. You can help me write this up."

"Hi, Gus. Bye, Gus."

"Hi, Miss Lily. Bye, Miss Lily." He chuckled.

As we made our way down to the basement cells, I texted Liv. *Are Will and James back yet?*

Yes. Everyone is safe and returned with their catches of the day. There was a laughing emoji and a fish emoji at the end. I laughed. Thank goodness today was another success. At least I could better focus on writing this one up now that I didn't have to worry.

When we were done, we went out to check on the squirrels. Tomorrow was the day, and we needed to run through everything again, just to make sure. Imani, of course, hadn't forgotten my tardiness returning. "So, what happened?"

"There were two guys out there."

She looked at me, realisation dawning in her expression. "Oh, and you considered for a loooooong moment on staying there and catching them?"

"Yes. But it was only for a moment. I made the sensible decision. See, I'm here, and they're not."

"You know Angelica, Will, James, your mum, they all would've skinned you alive."

"Well, what's the point of surviving it then? Maybe I should've stayed and taken those guys out. Besides, it wasn't that hard. I was going to hide behind the door and pretend I'd left, then build a doorway around them as soon as they walked in."

We reached the park bench, and as Imani opened her mouth to likely tell me off, I made my shrill whistle, then yelled, "Team Turmoil! We're back!"

Imani gave me an unimpressed glare. I gave her a "whadda ya gonna do?" look.

"I made the sensible decision. Okay? And before you say anything else, don't tell me you wouldn't have been tempted. That would've been two dangerous witches we wouldn't have had to deal with later."

She cocked her head to one side. "Tempted, probably, but would I ever consider it? Never. I'm trained to resist urges. If it's not an order, it doesn't happen. Ever."

"I'm not a trained agent, and this is why I'd make a terrible agent."

She gave me a weird look. I wasn't quite sure what it meant, and I didn't want to ask. Besides, the horde was arriving. I grinned. All my gorgeous squirrels. "Hello, everyone!"

Imani and I handed out nuts, then got to work. When we were finishing up, Angelica came down to see us.

"You ladies are hard at work, I see."

My stomach dropped. I would bet all the future double-chocolate muffins I would eat that she was here to see the squirrels' progress, then choose the ten she wanted. Imani answered, "Yes, Ma'am." I didn't have the words. And it was all my fault.

"So, show me what they can do."

I swallowed. "Grey the Brave, please take this explosive device and stick it on the front door." I handed him a small pebble that had one sticky side. He ran to the door of the temporary building, stuck it on the bottom, and ran straight back. "Good boy!" I handed him a peanut.

Thank you.

"Right, good. Can they all do that? We'll need ten at once for all the windows and doors on that side of the house."

"Yes. Watch." I looked at my squirrels and named ten of them—not Grey, but ten others—and they all came to me. Imani and I gave them each a pebble, and each of them was told a specific window or door to target. Off they went. Each one did the right thing and returned.

"Good squirrels!" They each got a nut.

We showed Angelica another drill where the squirrels snuck up on the security cameras, then squished a small ball of magical putty on there. It expanded and covered the lens in opaque, black film. "It'll get through the magic-seeking barriers and alarms because the magic is inactive until the ball is squished, then the spell is triggered."

"That's impressive, Lily. Did you come up with that?"

Imani and I looked at each other. "It was a joint effort. Imani thought of it and started the process, and when she couldn't quite make it work, I tweaked something, and voila. So it was mainly Imani." I grinned at her.

"Thanks, love. It was definitely a joint effort."

"Meh, you would've come up with the solution eventually. We just didn't have time, and I got lucky." They both looked at me as if to say, hmm, lucky. Yeah right.

"Well, ladies, it looks as if your crew is ready. So, I have these for them." Angelica held her hands up, and a small pile of black vests appeared in her cupped palms.

I sucked in a breath and picked one up. "Oh my God! It's a little bulletproof vest. They say Team Turmoil. Thank you!"

Her cheeks hitched up in a smile. "My pleasure. They can't wear them when they're planting the explosives, though, but when they come back, we can put them on them." She turned to the squirrels. "Welcome to the team, little ones. We're honoured to have you working with us." Well, that was something I never thought I'd see. Angelica addressing squirrels as if they were people.

The squirrels sent back joyous emotions and pride. A few little thank-yous were in there too. Tears tickled the corners of my eyes. My babies were ready, and I wished they weren't. If they didn't all come back safely, I didn't know how I'd deal with the guilt and the sorrow. They were all important to me now I'd gotten to know them.

"What time are we leaving tomorrow?" I asked.

"Four in the morning. We're going to get all this set up before sunrise. The best time to attack is when they're deep asleep and disoriented."

"But the guards will be awake, no doubt." Surely it wouldn't be that easy.

"Yes, of course, dear. But they won't take notice of a few squirrels, and if everyone else is asleep, we might kill a couple of the Cozzolino family in the explosions with a bit of luck. If only we could drop a bomb on their compound." Ah, there she was—bloodthirsty Angelica. The agent I knew and loved.

"If only," Imani agreed.

Did they have children? Surely Angelica didn't plan on killing them if they did. "Um, how old is the head of the witch mafia?"

"He's sixty-eight. His wife is sixty-seven. His son lives there, too, and he's forty-five. His wife is thirty-seven."

Don't ask, Lily. Don't ask. "Are there kids there." *Argh, damn you, brain!*

She gave me an insulted look. "What kind of monster do you think I am? The son has no children. That's why we decided to attack their compound. There won't be any innocents getting in the way like there would be out on the street. Cozzolino's brother lives there, but his wife died, and his kids moved away. They managed to escape the family business, which is a hard thing to do, and kudos to them."

"Right, okay. Thanks."

She stared at me, her poker face back. "You know, Lily, that even if there were children there, it wouldn't stop us. We might have changed up our plan of attack, but we need to bring these monsters down. All our lives are at stake. It's a risk we would've had no choice but to take if there was no better option."

"We need to cut the head off the snake." Imani's voice was strong, certain. She was right, of course.

"Once we've done that, the remaining members of the group will be easier to apprehend. We've arrested so many of them now that they're already in disarray. Once their leader is taken, they'll be in full panic mode, and there'll be no one organised enough to call the shots. It's almost as much fun as lining those dominoes up and pushing them over." Angelica smiled. I didn't mistake her joking around for lack of caution. None of us were under any illusions about how dangerous this was going to be. There was no point harping on it.

I turned to my squirrels. "Okay, guys. I'll see you bright and early tomorrow morning." This time I filled up their little troughs with nuts so all of them could eat, and I cuddled GTB goodbye. "See you soon, little buddy."

Bye, Lily.

Angelica handed me and Imani all the little vests. "You can do the honours tomorrow. I'm off to a meeting. Go home, relax, have an early night. Tomorrow's going to be a huge day."

"Okay." I waved goodbye as she walked off. I stared at the adorable, tiny bulletproof vests in my hands. What the hell had I done?

<h1 style="text-align:center">CHAPTER 12</h1>

Oh, the horror of getting out of bed at 3:30 a.m. At least Will and I were staying together today. I hadn't seen much of him at all the past few days. Once we were both dressed, I gave him a hug. "I've missed you."

He kissed the top of my head. "When this is all over, we'll finally go to Australia and get married." I could hear the smile in his voice as he held me tight. "I can't wait to see where you came from, and I expect you to show me a good time."

"I'm sure I can meet those expectations." I turned my face up to him, stood on my tippy toes, and kissed him. "Ooh, you shaved. Nice and smooth." He looked hot with a bit of stubble, but whenever I kissed him, my skin looked as if I'd dragged my face along gravel. Could someone be allergic to facial hair?

"I like to keep my lady happy." He kissed me again. "Stay safe today. Okay?"

"You too. I'm worried about my squirrels." It was stupid,

but tears burned my eyes. "What if one of them gets killed? It's all my fault they're going to be there."

He looked down at me and put his hands on my shoulders. "They'll be fine. They'll be in and out before anyone even notices them. Okay?"

"Okay." I wasn't convinced, but I had no choice but to pretend it was going to be fine.

"Lily, stop stressing. This isn't your first day on the job. Compared to some other stuff we've done, this will be easy, and the squirrels will be safe. We're the ones planning this. We have the element of surprise, and we can always abort if we have to. But we won't. We've taken out a lot of their key personnel already."

"But Cozzolino's strong. That's what the booklet says. Him and his brother."

"We're stronger." He kissed me again. "We'd better get going. Have faith. We're going to smash this… literally."

"If you say so." I gave him a resigned smile, but it was time to get out of my own head and focus. I had a super important job to do—keep my squirrels alive.

It was too early to eat—my body wasn't ready, and if I had a coffee now, I'd be busting to go to the toilet within fifteen minutes, and we didn't have time for that. Hopefully this wouldn't take more than an hour or two, and I'd be back in time for my morning coffee. Will made the doorway straight from the bedroom, and I went through first.

A different guard opened the door. Gus must still be asleep at home. Lucky sod. Will strode down the hallway next to me. "I'm coming with you to the squirrels."

"Nice. You can meet them all before we go."

"Sounds good."

HQ was eerily quiet. We were open twenty-four hours a

day, but staff were usually on call from home. Other than the guards and the witches manning the cells, there wasn't much to do at this hour. The poor squirrels. They weren't usually up this late, sensible creatures that they were.

When we went out there, I knew which trees each squirrel slept in. Rather than whistle and disturb all of them, I went to the different trees and called them down in a reasonable voice. It took a little longer—a few of them were sound sleepers— but soon, I had my ten squirrels. As I rounded up the last one, Imani, Angelica, James, Millicent, Beren, Sarah, and Lavender joined us.

Grey the Brave had claimed his spot on my shoulder, and Hamstring was on Imani's shoulder. She'd really taken to him, and every time I saw them together, I smiled. It was the small things… literally.

"Good morning, dear, Imani." Angelica smiled. "I thought I'd introduce everyone to our little army, so the squirrels felt more comfortable and knew who were the good guys and who weren't."

"That's a great idea." I turned to the eight squirrels who were on the ground. "Okay, guys, these are the PIB agents. These people are your friends. If you need help, hide behind them, but be careful not to get stepped on." They stared up at me, their dark eyes focussed. I introduced the agents one by one. "It's okay if you can't remember all their names, but make sure you remember their faces or scents or whatever." Once I was done with the agents' names, I told everyone who the squirrels were. At this point, we probably all needed name tags.

Lavender looked at me. "So, they really know what they're doing?"

"Yep. Imani and I have been working with them intensely

for a few days. They're way smarter than people give them credit for."

"I don't know," said Will, "they're tree rats, and rats are pretty smart." Bloody cheeky fiancé.

Yes, we are smart. Don't make Lily sad. I love her. Grey the Brave chittered and stared at Will.

I gave him a "so there" look. "Be nice to my squirrel army, or you'll be the last person they save if it comes down to it."

Will put up his hands. "Fine. I was just kidding."

I put my hand up in front of GTB, and he high-fived me. Sarah laughed. "Never change, Lily." I smiled. We hadn't spent much time together recently, and I missed her and Lavender. If this could all be over already, then we could go grab a cocktail and chill.

Soon, Lily. Soon.

"Where are their jackets?" Angelica eyed the squirrels.

"I figured I'd magic them here rather than carry them."

"Do it now, and then we can get going. Contrary to what we usually do, I don't want anyone holding any spells when we get there—they'll see us glowing in their boundary cameras. We'll cover three sides of the property." She held out her palm, and earpieces appeared in it. She handed one to Will. "You, Lily, and Lavender will be together on the western boundary." She handed one to Imani. "You, Sarah, and Beren will be on the eastern boundary, and James, Millicent, and I will be at the front of the property. A high brick fence surrounds it, as you know, but our squirrel friends will have no problem climbing up and over. So we can see what's going on when they're in there, I'm going to attach tiny cameras to them." She looked at the squirrels. "I hope you don't mind. The cameras weigh practically nothing, and we'll attach them to a collar around your neck They're very comfortable. Millicent's dad designed them." One appeared in her hand. "Here, Grey the Brave, you can try one on first and let your team know if it's okay."

Angelica magicked it on him, and he stilled for a moment. He touched it with his front paws and moved his head from side to side. *It's fine. As long as I can take it off when we come home.*

"Of course. Now, Team Turmoil…" She'd adopted the name I'd given them, which made me smile. It also made Lavender chuckle and Millicent snort. "…here we go." She magicked the rest of the camera collars on, and I magicked a large black shoulder bag from my bedroom, which had all the bulletproof vests in it.

"Are we ready?" Angelica's firm voice gave me a shot of pep. Her poker face pushed aside for a confident we're-going-to-kill-this expression. Everyone answered in the affirmative, including the squirrels. "I'm making the doorway. It will drop us off about half a mile from the compound in a spot we set up earlier."

"Oh, um, can everyone take a squirrel, so they don't get hurt going through?" I'd taught them how to use a doorway, but the light wasn't great, and they mightn't see it since they didn't have the ability to see magic like we did.

Angelica nodded. "Of course."

"Okay, squirrels, choose someone and sit on their shoulder." Percy, who was a bit bigger than GTB, climbed up my leg and sat on my other shoulder. "Hey, buddy. Nice to have you on board."

A small female squirrel, who I'd named Fiona, braved Will's shoulder. He gave her a surprised look that softened, and I snorted. I'd make a squirrel lover out of him yet, and by the time he noticed, it'd be too late.

When the squirrels were all situated, none on her, Angelica

said, "Let's go." Looked like the squirrels were wary of our esteemed leader, and they probably should be. Maybe they could feel her no-nonsense vibes?

We stepped through onto the grass verge beside a dirt road on the side of a hill that I could just make out under the half-moon. The night was clear, and since we were in a country area, thousands of stars streaked across the night sky like silver paint splatter. The fresh air carried the unpleasant hint of cow manure. At least no one was likely to notice a few weird lightning strikes out here or hear the explosions. From the aerial view we'd seen of the compound, neighbours were few and far between.

Again, not accessing my powers sucked, and I was sweating in my jacket. My stomach gurgled, out of sorts. I swallowed my nerves. *We're going to win. Everything will be fine.* My squirrels would pick up on how I was feeling, so I needed to do everything I could to squash my fear.

No one spoke. The only sounds were our breathing, muffled bootsteps on the grass, and the droning of crickets. It could be any warm night in any countryside setting. But it wasn't. We weren't relaxed and strolling in the early morning.

We were marching to war.

Soon, Angelica stopped behind some bushes. She pointed across the road. The outline of the wall was barely discernible by sight, but I could feel its presence. Tall, impregnable, hiding a place we didn't need to know about. My eyes widened. I tapped Angelica on the shoulder and motioned for her to lean towards me. I whispered in her ear, "Is there a spell that makes us want not to go near it?"

She stared at me, then put her mouth to my ear. "Is your magic locked up?" I nodded. "Yet, you can still feel it?"

"I just know that I feel the barrier like a tangible thing that worries me, and that's not normally how I react to brick walls. I'm not sure if all the squirrels will want to climb it."

"They would've modified it for people only so that wildlife, bees, etcetera still visit. They have an orchard that would need bugs to survive. They also have dogs and chickens."

"Um, okay." Note to self: the squirrels might get attacked by dogs. "Do you know what sort of dogs?"

"A couple of yappy ones, but two rottweilers that accompany the guards." Of course they had two attack dogs. "Don't worry, dear, they're normally on leads and with someone. Your squirrels will be fine. Now, it's time. Dawn is approaching, and we need to get to it." She reached into her pocket and pulled something out. "Here are the balls of putty. Make sure you give one to each squirrel. When you're done, you need to go with Will, Lavender, and the three squirrels for that side of the house. When we're in position, I'll give the instructions to let the squirrels go. Good luck, Lily."

I nodded because my throat practically closed up with fear for my little guys and, if I was being honest, us as well. I handed all the putty out to Team Turmoil with reminder instructions, then returned to Will. The sweet girl on his shoulder could come with us. I whispered to him, "Angelica's asked us to get into position." I then went to Lavender and put my lips to his ear. "Please give your squirrel to James. We're getting into position now. Oh, and give him these jackets to hand out." He gave a nod. I handed him the jackets and his squirrel the putty, reminded it what it was supposed to do, and Lavender ran it all over to James.

I gave our three remaining squirrels the putty and instructions. Our little group bent low and hurried across the road and along the eastern part of the boundary. About forty feet along, a tall tree grew about six feet from the fence. It was perfect for the squirrels to jump to the top of the fence from. They would have no trouble fitting through the layers of barbed wire atop it. We'd trained them on how to avoid the sharp bits.

After being there for a minute, James whispered, "Go time."

The slight weight of the squirrels disappeared from my shoulders as they jumped to the tree. As they scurried up it, I shivered. It wasn't just fear for them, but the proximity to the fence that screamed "beware" and "go away." What did the locals think of the place? Was there a rumour it was haunted or something? At least they wouldn't get door-to-door salesmen or religious fanatics on a conversion bender.

I bit my thumbnail. The squirrels disappeared over the top of the fence. I stared at the spot and took deep breaths. *Please be okay.* Lavender kept a watch on our surroundings, and I listened as hard as I could for footsteps, shouting, barking, or squirrels screaming. *Ouch*! I'd bitten too much of my nail, and it ripped off skin. I sucked my thumb. Crap.

Waiting was the worst. My squirrels must've reached the house by now and were probably finding their assigned windows or doors. The model house we'd built at HQ had a similar layout to this building, albeit our version was smaller. At least there hadn't been any kerfuffle yet.

I looked at Will. He could've been a garden statue, standing so still, awaiting Angelica's instructions. Mum and Liv were at HQ watching the monitors with the squirrel feed on them. When all the squirrels had done their jobs and gotten to the compound boundary wall, it would be time to let our minibombs do their work.

We were standing here to make sure no one escaped or snuck around after the explosions happened, but once we'd made sure of that, we were to enter the compound via the front gates, which would also be blown to smithereens. They were heavy timber that you couldn't see through. The squirrels had been warned to stay away from them when escaping.

What was that? My gaze pinged to the top of the fence. Movement. I sucked in a deep breath. Two of my squirrels jumped across to the tree. Where was the third?

Will's girl jumped from the tree trunk to his shoulder. The next was Percy. He came and stood near me. *Come on, Grey. Where are you?* There! He climbed through the barbed wire and leaped to the tree. My racing heart slowed. Now they were here, I grabbed three little jackets out of my bag and put them on the squirrels. Oh my God, talk about adorable.

Grey the Brave looked down at it, then up at me. His little chest puffed up. A feeling of invincibility washed over me. I knelt on the ground and whispered to him, "That only stops bullets. You still need to be careful."

His large eyes stared at my face. After a few beats, he nodded. *I understand.* I smiled and stood. Now that my crew was safe, I could go back to staring at Will, waiting for confirmation to move.

Will raised his hand as if to say he was listening. After a bit, he nodded, then covered his ears. Lavender and I did the same, and I readied to open to the river of magic. Whatever came next, it was going to be chaos, and it was going to happen quickly.

My stomach tensed. I pushed my hands over my ears tighter. If only we were privy to a countdown.

Light flashed, illuminating the hillside, the trees, and the wall before going dark. A boom sounded, glass smashed, the thuds of debris hitting the ground and crashing against the fence filled the early morning. The squirrels hid behind the tree. An orange ball of fire whooshed into the sky. An alarm squealed, and men shouted.

Will said, "Magic, now!"

I opened the portal, and power filled me. And it filled a whole lot of other people too. Different magics zinged and prickled my scalp and nape. I shuddered, goosebumps springing up along my arms. I recognised some of them, but there were many I didn't.

Smoke stung my eyes and wafted up my nose. Lightning cracked and exploded within the perimeter of the property.

Will turned to me. "Angelica wants you out the front. Lavender and I will stay here for two more minutes; then we'll join you. Hurry!"

I didn't wait to be told twice. I sprinted along the fence line, turned left at the corner, and bolted to Angelica. James, Millicent, and Imani were with her. Squirrels wearing their Team Turmoil jackets hovered around behind them on the grass, wisely keeping out of the way.

The front gates were in pieces strewn about, some of it even on the road and across the road. Sheesh, whatever magic was in that putty was lethal. The massive home visible through the gaping hole in the fence—some of the bricks had disintegrated with the fence—was on fire. Men ran towards us, their auras sparking with magic, the two rottweilers at their heels.

"Looks like they're coming to us. Are they really going to make it this easy?"

"Look closer, dear."

Dammit. They all had on shields and return to senders.

"Now what? We rumble?" Those guys would squash me. There were five of them, and they were huge. Not to mention the dogs. I turned to the squirrels. "Run away. There are dogs. Find a tree and hide!" Thank the universe they listened to me and bounded away across the road and to a row of pencil conifers.

"Pay attention, dear. Things are about to get messy. Hold your shield tight."

My eyes widened. The men had stopped forty feet away, forming a wall with their bodies. One of them pulled out a bazooka. What. The. Hell? "Can our shields withstand that?"

"I don't know. We've never tried." Way to go, Angelica.

"So, why are we just standing here?"

"Hold hands, everyone. Lily's going to join our power."

We stood in a circle and linked hands. "I'm ready." They threw their power to me, and I made a shield that covered all of us, like a snow globe, but without the pretty white bits. As long as we weren't shaken like one, we'd survive this.

Did I want to watch it hit? Yeah, nah, but I had no choice. "As soon as it hits, we attack them."

Angelica stared at me, but I turned my head to face our enemies. One of them knelt on the ground, the bazooka on his shoulder.

Crap.

It was hard to even react when it came out of the tube. It happened in a nanosecond.

It slammed into our shield. I gasped as pain shot through my stomach. The impact was like being crushed by a building. We staggered back but managed to keep our hands linked. Not doing so would've been fatal. I looked down, and even though my innards felt like they were spilling out onto the ground, my stomach was intact. That was brutal.

We had to put everything into our retaliation, so it didn't come back to us. I needed to break their return to senders. "Lightning. Attack!" I screamed. I sucked everyone's power into me until I couldn't channel any more. I dropped our shield and called down fork lightning. Oh my God, it even looked like a giant fork. Skewering four of the men, tearing right through their shields. I threw up our bubble as soon as I'd released our power, but Angelica was panting, and sweat poured off my face and into the space between my boobs. Millicent grunted.

"Lily, they're down!" James panted out, exhausted but exhilarated. "There's one left, and he's running away." The dogs lay dead. I was kind of sorry, but not. They were trained to kill. It wasn't their fault, but better them than me. That made me horrible, but I'd have to live with it.

We dropped hands. "Don't lose concentration." Angelica spoke into her earpiece. "Everyone, gather at the front. Run!" She pulled a gun out of her jacket. Whoa, this was getting serious. She rarely used a gun, but I'd drained everyone's magic. Dammit. Was that our first big mistake? She turned to James. "Check those bodies. Identify them for me." Beren reached us. "Go with him. Cover."

"Yes, Ma'am."

They warily entered the grounds, then bolted to the bodies. James photographed the blackened corpses. Would their smoking remains even be identifiable? I needed to find a different way of killing people, one that left more... person.

We watched them, and I was ready to use my magic again. I wasn't as tired as everyone else. Despite the ache in my stomach, I hadn't used my own power... much. I wasn't exhausted yet. While they were in there, everyone else arrived. I sent the rest of the squirrels to the trees across the road. Grey the Brave tried to argue. "If you're here, I'll worry about you. Please just go. It'll mean I can concentrate on what I need to."

But you need me. I know you still do.

"I need you alive. That's what I need. Now, go."

I swore his little forehead wrinkled. He wasn't happy. His tail twitched angrily, but he turned and bounded across the road. At least I could concentrate on only the humans now.

James and Beren returned. More shouts came from the compound. More magic scraped along my scalp. "Someone else is drawing magic. It feels… powerful and cruel."

Angelica frowned. "Our explosions didn't kill Cozzolino, then. We need to go in and find him before he escapes."

"You don't think he'll attack us?" James asked.

"Lily, can you throw a no-leave spell over the house?"

I sucked in a breath. "What? That's… huge."

"I'll help." Imani grabbed my hand.

"So will I." Sarah clutched my other hand.

"Okay. Let's do this." They drew power from the river and sent it to me. I syphoned as much as I could, then made the spell and imagined it falling over the house like a fishing net. "Done." I tied it off. Maintaining it would take some of my power, but I could manage for half an hour or so.

"Thank you, ladies. Okay, search formation now. Return to senders and shields up. If you can't manage it, stay here." As she moved towards the property, everyone went with her, including me. I felt vulnerable out here by myself. My luck would be that they see me alone and come get me. Yeah, no thanks.

Everyone had their guns drawn. No gun for me. Oh well. I'd probably accidentally shoot myself with it, so that was fine. As we jogged along the driveway, a man screamed. It sounded like an angry scream, a scream of the wild. I smiled. That was probably our target realising he couldn't escape, or maybe he just discovered that many of his men were dead.

"Fan out. Expect to meet resistance." The house loomed in front of us, and Angelica moved out to the right, Beren,

Lavender, and Imani going with her. I veered left to go around the side and make sure no one was making a break for it over any fences. Will was behind me. Everyone else went towards the front door, which was basically just a hole in the wall.

The chaos of glass, bricks, and rubble strewn across the ground meant I had to watch where I placed my feet. I was doubly glad my squirrels weren't in here—they could easily cut a paw or worse.

Much of my concentration was taken by watching where I was walking, and before I knew it, I'd reached the back of the house. I looked up. The night sky had lightened slightly, giving the home an ominous feel with its noticeably blown-out, dark window holes that no longer reflected anything. The back door was intact because we weren't going to enter through there, and no one would've likely been anywhere near it, although it was already open.

I turned to ask Will what we should do, but he wasn't with me. Oh, okay. Not a problem. Not much was going on out the back. I might as well stay here, just in case, and because it was quiet, I was safe… for now. I kept my gaze on the windows and doorway. My return to sender and shield were up, but how long they'd last if I was attacked, I had no idea. Tiredness flitted around the edges. I'd built up stamina since I'd been in England, but I still had my limit.

Shouting came from the front of the property, and magic tingled my scalp. Angelica and Imani, but there were two other lots of magic I didn't recognise. Still, I stayed where I was. If everyone wasn't drawing magic, it probably wasn't that bad. And maybe our enemies wanted to lure me away from here so they could try to escape.

And now there was another noise coming from behind me. I spun around. The choppy whine of a helicopter. What? Had the police or fire brigade come to check what was going on? I supposed that explosion and subsequent fire would've looked like a potential forest fire, and it was the end of the hot, dry season.

Behind me was a magnificent rectangular pool, and beyond that, from what I could see, was one of the tennis courts. The blinking lights on the descending helicopter seemed to be aiming for ground beyond that. Ah, that's right; there was a helipad here. Of course there was. Rich people and their extravagant lives. When we'd looked at the aerial shots, I'd been more interested in the fact there was more than one pool and more than one tennis court.

The noise got louder, and as the helicopter came close to the ground, the breeze found me. Dust blew into my eyes and mouth. I turned around and blinked and spat. Ew. *Crap, get out of my mouth.*

Oh. A large man stood on the back terrace. Where had his imposing six foot five, broad-shouldered, muscular frame come from? He must've exited the house before I'd spelled it. Crap. He was three times my bulk and carried a duffel bag in one hand and a gun in the other. His gaze clung to me, and my stomach twisted.

Cozzolino.

His teeth glowed white in a blood-chilling smile. "Ah, you're the famous Lily Bianchi." Instead of sounding sexy, his raspy, deep Italian-accented voice made me shudder. He wasn't a romantic hero but a psychopath who hurt people to make money.

"And you're the loser who tied their boat to the wrong mooring." Hmm, that wasn't a very powerful metaphor. Meh, I'd do better next time. It was the word "loser" that got his attention, though. He'd probably stopped listening after that.

He strode towards me, his long legs covering the ground quickly. I forced my feet to stay where they were. Showing fear was the worst thing I could do now, and I'd bet he fed off that. I was just glad he couldn't hear my rapid heartbeat. We both had shields up, so the worst he could do to me was push me over. If he tried to stab or shoot me, he'd have to let his shield down. Hmm, if he got close enough, I could potentially cuff him.

He stopped a few feet from me. "I'm sorry I can't stop to chat, but I have a helicopter to catch." He pointed his gun at my head. I did my best to appear unruffled.

"Overcompensating?"

He gave me a confused look. Okay, so I was going to have to spell it out for him.

I sighed, held up my pinky finger, and wriggled it. "Overcompensating. You know." Maybe chuckling was going too far, but his horrified face was priceless.

Anger took over, and he closed the distance between us in four stomps. He pushed the gun up to my temple, but I couldn't feel it because my shield was in the way. "You play a dangerous game, Miss Bianchi. I could end your life right now if I so chose."

"Why don't you? Come on. Here I am." I waited a few beats, my pulse throbbing in my neck. "Oh, that's right. My magic is stronger than yours. You'll never get a bullet through my shield. Sucks to be you."

His dark eyes bulged. I could feel the pressure from him pressing hard on my shield. I resisted the urge to shut my eyes. I stared into his and silently dared him, hoping it came through my gaze. In a fraction of a second, he dropped his shield, shot three times, the sound cracking like a whip, and erected his shield. I staggered back two steps, pain slicing through my stomach and eardrums. Shields didn't protect against sound, apparently. The whole thing had taken me by surprise, and I missed an opportunity to hurt him. My shield held, but my breaths came faster, and tiredness crept in around the edges, along with a headache. How many more bullet hits could I take? I stood straight and pretended nothing had happened.

He flicked his gaze towards the house, then turned towards me and spat on the ground. "Bah, you're not worth my time." He gave up easily. Maybe I was stronger than he originally thought. Did normal witches die by the second shot at close range? He must've assumed it was going to take ages to hurt me, and the sound of shots must've caught the attention of one of my friends. He was happy to face me alone but not a few of us.

He strode towards the helicopter without a backward glance. Well, that was anticlimactic. Not that I wanted him standing there shooting me until my shield collapsed, but why wasn't he trying to finish me off?

I wasn't going to let him get away. I grabbed my handcuffs from my inside jacket pocket and readied to put them on his wrist. I'd have quite a fight once he realised what I intended, but I had to try. I quietly jogged behind him and caught up. With the cacophony of the helicopter, I was silent like a ninja. I held the cuffs in front of me, and when his left arm swung back towards me, I snapped the cuff on it because his shield was moulded to his body rather than in a dome—it took way less energy, and I didn't know how easy it was to hold a dome shield while you were moving. He stopped and jerked towards me, swinging me around in the process. If I let go of the other cuff, that would be the end of that arrest, and the last thing we needed was for him to get one of our cuffs and figure out how they worked.

"*Merda!* Get off me." He jerked his arm, shaking me and my bag. I gritted my teeth and gripped harder.

"No. You're under arrest." Okay, so that was a stretch, but I wasn't giving up. Surely someone else would come along soon and help. Didn't anyone hear those shots? Even if I wanted to scream for help, no one would hear me. Why couldn't something go right?

He kept going. I continued trying to drag his arm towards the other one, but it was futile. What the hell was I thinking? I was ineffectual at best, and really, at this point, it was safe to say I was an embarrassment.

As if he'd read my mind, he laughed. "They said you were a powerful witch. The price on your head is one I would like to claim. You can come with me." He slid his gun into his pants, and I hoped he accidentally blew his jewels off. Then he picked me up under one arm as if I were a small rug. This was ridiculous. I hadn't released the handcuff, though.

We reached the helicopter. Oh, God, I'd better think of something quickly, or I was going for a ride, and helicopters scared me. Small and likely to crash into wires—death traps if you asked me. Also, this was getting more 007 by the moment. Mafia, Tuscan compounds, guns, and helicopters. Where was MI6 when you needed them?

And, oh, my stupid, stupid brain. I should've let him get in the damn death trap and just shot it out of the sky with lightning. Why was I so stupid? Honestly, why Angelica let me near any investigations was beyond me. I was clearly unfit for duty. Although, if he was as powerful as Angelica said, he could've put a return to sender around the aircraft. It would've been possible to hold it at least until they were out of range of my magic.

He climbed into the helicopter and threw me into a plush seat. It was like no helicopter I'd ever imagined. It had a carpeted floor and white leather seats. It was basically a flying limo. The pilot looked over his shoulder, his eyes widening. His aura told me he wasn't a witch. Hmm, how could I use that to my advantage?

Cozzolino slammed the door shut, and his magic scraped my scalp. The pilot now had a shield as well. Crap, but also, he was spreading his magic out, which would make him slightly weaker. It could mean the difference between who of us won in a magic stoush. But if I beat him—either got that handcuff on the other wrist or killed him—would the pilot do as I asked? Did he have a gun? It wasn't as if I would kill the pilot —I had no idea how to fly a helicopter.

As the helicopter rose, I gripped the other handcuff. There was no way I was getting it on him. What the hell had I gotten myself into?

Cozzolino laughed and looked at my hand. He had to yell to be heard over the spinning blades. "You going to let go? We both know you're never getting that other cuff on me. Give up."

I pressed my lips together, fighting the urge to cry. Frustration bubbled inside me. This piece of crap wasn't getting away with anything. The directors weren't going to win. This wasn't just about me but about everyone they'd ever wronged. The scum of the earth weren't allowed to get away with the evil they'd been perpetrating. When did Karma get her day?

If I had my way, it would be today.

Cozzolino smirked, then put his earphones and mouthpiece on. He yanked his hand and jerked me to the side, then laughed. He put his hand in his lap, and I had to lean over to accommodate it. Jerk. I narrowed my eyes. *Ooh, you're going to get it, buddy. Top. Of. My. List.*

The only question was, how?

We both had return to senders and shields. Even if we didn't have shields, there was no way I could hurt him by punching him. He could just sit on me, and that would be the end of it. At least there was no way he could undo the hand-cuffs. Hmm…. If I could get him to drop all his protections, I could hit him hard and fast. I'd have the advantage.

That gave me an idea.

I eyed the rectangular handle sticking out of the wall to his right. It looked like it was for holding on when getting in and out of the helicopter. I couldn't cast magic directly onto Cozzolino, but I'd bet I could cast magic on the side of the cuff I was touching. I imagined it locked onto the handle and added a protection spell to the handle and wall around it so that if he tried to undo it, the helicopter would end up with a hole in it. I made it obvious that it would take a hell of a long time to unravel. The rest of my plan was going to be a work in progress, but this should get things started.

I dropped my protection spells, which he didn't realise because he wasn't looking at me, and I quickly drew power from the river and let go of the handcuff. *Please work.* I released the spell as he turned to me with his mouth in a huge O.

I reinstated my previous spells and grinned. He was leaned over as far as he could go, his left wrist clipped onto the wall handle in front and to his right. Victory! It was a small victory, but a victory nonetheless. I wanted to scream "sucked in," but he wouldn't hear me over the helicopter. More's the shame. Instead, when he turned his head awkwardly to glare spewing lava at me, I stuck my middle finger up. Ah, so satisfying.

He tried to wrench his arm and cuff off the handle. Not happening. He screamed, and the pilot spun around to look at him. He would've gotten an earful through his headset. As long as he didn't crash the helicopter. Yikes.

The pilot said something into his mouthpiece. I had no idea what. The mafia boss replied, then spat at me. Ew, gross. "You have no manners." I knew he couldn't hear me, but maybe he'd be wondering what I'd said. "You're going down." I had to admit that it was hard to goad someone into a mistake when they couldn't hear you. He still had his protection spells. Surely it would only be a matter of time until he tried to remove himself from the cuffs with magic. What else could I do to provoke him? I also needed to hurry up because we'd probably soon be wherever it was we were going.

Hmm. I didn't want to drain myself too much, but I was going to try and destroy the protection spell on the pilot. Not that I'd do anything to him because I didn't want to die in a fiery helicopter crash. But he didn't know how crazy I was or wasn't.

I dropped my shield. This was probably a bad idea, but I didn't know what else to hit him with, seeing as how I didn't know how to suck enough heat out of the air around me to create a fireball. Also, fire probably wasn't good for the helicopter. I chose a small lightning bolt. The problem was it came in via the windscreen, slicing a hole in it and cracking the rest of it.

When the lightning hit the pilot, even though he was protected, he was forced back in his seat as if someone had shoved him. Cozzolino stared at me, his face twisted in fury. But my shield was back up. I smiled and waved, and then I figured putting a cherry on top wouldn't hurt, so I waggled my eyebrows up and down.

That did the trick. He lunged for me, but the handcuffs stopped him. He moved his whole upper body, trying to break them. Other than a slight tug in my stomach, it did nothing to further his goals.

"My magic isn't that strong, hey?" If only he could hear me. I looked around, but there weren't any other headsets, and I wasn't game to get next to him so I could yell in his ear. I was a bit dopey at times, but not that dopey.

The pilot kept glancing back at me, fear in his eyes. At least someone realised I was a danger to them. Meh, this was taking too long. I *was* actually going to be that dopey. But I had my spell on, so he couldn't hurt me. I stood, stooped over, and lifted his earphone off. He grabbed at me with his free hand and secured my wrist, but because he was twisted around, all I had to do was jerk my wrist out, and that would be that. I yelled in his ear. "Do you want to die, or will you let me put that handcuff on your other wrist and arrest you?"

He shouted, "You don't have the guts to die for your cause."

"You're going to kill me anyway, aren't you? You want that reward, and the directors will kill me once you hand me over, so my fate is sealed either way." My stomach somersaulted as that realisation hit. But then again, it wasn't over till it was over, and I still had access to my powers. I could make a doorway at any time and be gone. *Oh my God, that was it.* "Actually, I don't plan on going down with this contraption. So, what will it be?"

"What, you're going to grow wings? If we duelled magic to magic, you'll die." His eyes brightened. "Ah, but I can still collect my money, even if you're dead." He dropped his protection spells and grinned. "Oh, don't tell me you're too scared. Ha, I knew it!" He drew magic and started to unravel my spell that kept him chained. He couldn't unravel it without looking at it, and he needed to keep an eye on me as well to see when I dropped my spells. Ah, crap. Well, I could keep my return to sender up, but I needed to drop my shield. But as soon as I started drawing magic, he slammed his shields up. Right, a ridiculous game of chicken that no one could win.

My forehead tightened. Had we started descending? Damn it. Right. I had no choice. It was time to act. *Come on, brain.* I snatched my arm out of his grasp and went to my chair. I swallowed as an idea came to me. I could make a doorway around the helicopter and take it to the place we'd landed—it was close… well, closer than HQ. But I'd never tried to translocate anything this big before. Could I even make a doorway that big? It would take an enormous amount of power and control, probably more than I had.

Crap. There was only one other thing to do.

I dropped my shield and sucked in as much power as I could. Cozzolino stared at me and licked his lips. He dropped his shield and lunged again, but the cuffs held fast. He got to work unravelling my spell. My blood heated, and sweat slicked my forehead and under my arms. This was it. I called a large lightning bolt from the sky. It exploded through the windshield, killing the pilot instantly. His hands fell off the controls, and the chopper skewed to one side and dropped.

I let one more spell fly at the cuffs, melting them to the handle. Cozzolino stared at me, terror in his eyes. The chopper fell faster. It would smash into the ground soon, but I had to time my exit and make sure he had no way to save himself.

"You lose." I readied my doorway around myself but didn't put the destination in yet. I was leaning to one side, staring out the window at the lights of a cluster of homes off to the side. We weren't going to land on them, but it would be close. My stomach fell as if it was on the worst roller-coaster of my life as we plummeted.

I glanced at Cozzolino, who, in his panic, wasn't thinking. For a crafty mafia dude, he was a disappointment. He ripped his body back and forth, trying to dislodge himself. When that didn't help, he tried to cut the handle from the helicopter with heat. It wasn't working.

With my heartbeat racing out of control and my mouth dry, I glanced out the window. Crap. Time was up.

I slammed the coordinates on my doorway and shut my eyes.

"Oof!" I landed on my bottom, pain jarring along my back. That'd teach me to make a doorway around myself when I was seated with my eyes closed. I opened my eyes. I was alive! Yes! And in the spot that we'd landed in before walking to the Cozzolino compound. I slid my phone from my inside jacket pocket and called Angelica. Hopefully she wasn't in the middle of hiding, although she'd have her phone on silent.

"Lily! Where the hell are you?" Okay, so that wasn't her usual cool, calm, and collected phone voice.

"I'm down the road a bit, where the doorway is, and I'm fine. I do have some news, though." Would she be angry that I'd killed him? At least, I thought I'd killed him. What if he'd survived?

"Get your behind back to the compound, now. We'll talk when you get here." She hung up. Okay, so maybe she hadn't been that worried about me. She was probably just angry because I went off and did my own thing. Even if she was worried, I was getting a lecture either way. I could feel it coming.

I stood and dusted myself off. Hmm, my bag was still over

my shoulder. I started to laugh at the absurdity of that, but then I remembered that my first official pair of PIB handcuffs were lost forever. I'd melted them, and now they probably, hopefully, had Cozzolino's blood all over them. Hmm, did I detect a hint of Angelica in that thought?

Halfway to the lights and noise of the compound, my army met me. They swarmed up my arms and legs, clung to my shirt and jacket, and sat on my shoulders and head. An overwhelming sensation of chills and heat—fear, worry, and love—cascaded over me. Little voices invaded my head. *Are you okay?*

We thought you'd been killed.

Are you hurt?

Where did you go?

Do you have any nuts?

I chuckled. "Ah, Dusty, don't ever change. Actually...." I smiled. There had been a good reason I'd saved that bag. And it wasn't as empty as I'd thought. I reached in and pulled out the packet of nuts I'd brought for when the job was done. I was handing out the last of the nuts to my literal hangers-on when I reached the compound. I felt like a Christmas tree with living baubles. They were light by themselves, but pile them on, and they made walking harder.

Angelica stood on the road, feet planted wide, arms folded. She was trying to glare, but her eyes narrowed. She burst out laughing. "What in the world?"

Will and James, who'd been standing a few feet away talking, noticed me. They both jogged over. "Lily! Where the hell have you been?" Will stood in front of me, trying to find a gap to hug me through my furry accessories. He gave up.

James frowned. "Where were you? You had us all worried sick."

"I think I killed Cozzolino. You'd need to check."

Angelica stared into the distance. We were at a high point, and there was glowing many miles away on lower land. "So, you were in the helicopter too?"

"I assume that's the burning wreckage?" I'd been so close to being in that scorching fireball.

"Yes, dear."

"Yes. I'm pretty sure Cozzolino went down with it, but I got out just before it crashed. He was handcuffed to the handrail when I left." I sort of felt guilty for the pilot, but then again, get in bed with the mafia, you get what you get.

Grey the Brave, who was one of two squirrels on my left shoulder, nuzzled his face against mine. Oh my God, the cuteness. I turned my face and touched noses. The squirrel on my head bent over and touched its nose to my forehead. I laughed. Will sighed, and James shook his head.

"Lily!" Sarah called out and ran towards us. She reached me and laughed. "You seem to be covered by an infestation of squirrels. Is that what happened? Were you squirrelnapped?"

"Not quite." Angelica's voice was not amused. "She went off without telling anyone, and it could've ended very badly." She turned to James. "I've already called the others. They should be at HQ by now."

I looked around. "Um, where are the criminals? Didn't you arrest anyone?"

"They're back in lock-up, dear. We only ended up with four. The rest were eliminated… not intentionally, but it seems you're not the only one with a penchant for messing up arrests." She looked at James again. "We need to confirm Cozzolino's demise. Can you take Will and get there now, before his men figure out what's happened?"

"Yes, Ma'am." James turned and looked at me. "Never do that again. You never go off without telling anyone."

Shame burnt my cheeks. "I didn't mean to. Sheesh. It kind of happened quickly. When I first went around the back, I thought Will was with me."

"So you're telling me that at no time could you have called one of us or ran back around the front? You had all your protection spells, no?"

I pouted for a moment. My brother knew me so well. "Yes, but—"

He held his hand up in a stop motion. "No. I don't want to hear it. If I had to go back and tell Mum I'd let you get killed.... Just don't do it again. Understood?"

I sighed. "I don't know. I'll try not to." Well, he wanted me to tell the truth. I knew myself, and even though I had the best of intentions, intentions seemed to fly out the window when I was around.

His forehead wrinkled, and he looked to the heavens as if to say "see what I have to deal with. See?!" He looked at Ma'am. "We'll come straight back to headquarters when we're done."

She gave a nod. "Okay, team. Lily, you can make sure the squirrels get through the doorway."

Sarah counted. "You have them all." She giggled.

Will shook his head slowly, found a gap, and kissed me on the cheek. "Funnily enough, I'm not surprised." He gave me a lopsided grin, then followed James through a doorway.

Angelica smirked. "I think you've finally broken him, dear. That poor lad." She made her doorway and walked through.

Sarah grinned. "Don't worry, Lily. You haven't broken my brother. He secretly loves how crazy you drive him." She made her doorway and left.

"Right, squirrels, hang on tight and keep those tails in." I made a doorway twice as big as usual and left the smouldering ruins of a mafia family behind me.

One criminal group down, two to go. And all before sunrise.

CHAPTER 13

Before I wrote up my version of what happened with Cozzolino, I grabbed a coffee from the cafeteria. It was staffed twenty-four hours, thank goodness. Once I'd inhaled it and a cheese-and-ham croissant, I did the paperwork. All this paperwork lately was doing my head in. Angelica was trying to make sure our procedures made things clear for anyone from MI6 who came in and checked on things. After an hour of that, Will and James returned with Cozzolino's body and his pilot's in body bags. They'd documented everything, and a PIB crew had disposed of the evidence as the sun rose.

Now we all sat in the conference room with Agents Plover, Dupont, and Prentice. Angelica had just updated everyone on how many of our enemies we'd managed to arrest or kill. That number was rather large, and it made me feel better. We still had two smaller organisations to take down, but things were changing.

Angelica sat at the head of the table and folded her hands

on the desk in front of her. "The Cozzolino mafia organisation is no more. I'm sending some agents to clean up the last little pocket of them this morning. The rest will be cousins who have nothing to do with the day-to-day running of the organisation. We'll keep an eye on them, but they pose no real threat at the moment." Angelica looked around the table. "Thank you all for your work thus far. This morning went as well as we could've hoped, except for Agent Bianchi." No one was even confused about who she meant. All eyes turned to me, including Angelica's. "You didn't follow protocol."

I held my hand up but didn't wait for her to say okay. "But I don't even know what protocol is. No one ever told me."

"Common sense, dear. You should've called someone. The first we knew of the danger was the helicopter and gunshots. You shouldn't have taken him on by yourself." Her hard stare made me shuffle my bottom. I wanted to look away, but I didn't. It wouldn't have been as embarrassing if the MI6 agents weren't in the room. "However..." Oh, there was a however? "...you killed Cozzolino, by yourself." Her magic tingled my scalp, and paper appeared on the table under her hands. She picked it up. "In your report, you stated that he shot three bullets into your temple at point-blank range. Just for your information, only approximately 10 per cent of witch agents' magic would've protected against the third shot. Don't let it happen again, Lily." Oops, she'd slipped to my first name. "The outcome could've been far different. Am I understood?"

"Yes, Ma'am." I wanted to tell her that it wasn't as if I'd wanted to be shot in the head. I didn't ask for that situation, but I also had to admit that I figured my magic would protect me. The shots weakened me a little bit, but I was sure I could've withstood ten bullets at close range. Now wasn't the time to argue if I wanted the attention off me ASAP, so I kept quiet. Maybe if I didn't move, she'd forget I was here? Also, was that a look of sympathy from Agent Plover? How unexpected.

"And you can tell your squirrels what a great job they did. Team Turmoil's first operation was a success." She allowed a small smile to crack her façade for a few seconds before reinstating her poker face. I couldn't help smiling at that. They'd be so excited to receive that praise from the top. "I have another job for them tomorrow, but we'll discuss that later. Now, moving right along…." She turned to the MI6 agents, who sat next to each other on the opposite side of the table from where I sat in between Will and Liv. Another job so soon? Were we all taking down the second most powerful criminal group already? I guessed the sooner we did it, the better.

"Because we've been stretched thin and MI6 need our help protecting their agents from the rogue witches, we've decided, for the next week at least, to combine our agent pools. We're matching witch agents with MI6 non-witch agents. They'll be helping us with our work, and we'll be helping them in a swap-style arrangement. That will mean our cases continue to be dealt with in a timely manner, and their agents are safer on the job."

Agent Prentice nodded. "Thank you for working with us on this."

Angelica smiled. "It's the least we could do since your support has put your agents in the sights of the directors."

"True," the head of MI6 said. "But it might pave the way for new processes and certainly a closer collaboration between our organisations. Agent Bianchi's intervention in our cases this week has seen them solved quickly and efficiently. I dare say bringing your people in to help us will increase the safety of the United Kingdom and decrease our spending."

Imani put up her hand. "Yes, Agent Jawara?" Angelica said.

"I thought the idea was to introduce witches into MI6 anyway?"

"Yes, dear, it was. It's just happening much quicker and on a larger scale than we previously envisaged."

"Which is a good thing." Agent Prentice smiled.

Will chuckled. "Instead of destroying the PIB as the directors wanted, they've made us impressively stronger. We should thank them."

James frowned. "We have to catch them first... or kill them. Let's not celebrate too early." My brother's comment sobered everyone, dashing smiles from faces.

"Way to go, brother of mine. Don't we get a five-minute break from being stressed? Let us have a laugh, even if it's just a small one."

"Sorry, Lily, but we can't lose focus. We're so close."

"We are." Angelica smoothed her bun. "Tomorrow we're simultaneously going after the second-largest crime group and the directors."

My eyes widened. "But that's crazy! We don't have the resources. The directors are strong witches."

"Yes, dear, but we can't leave it any longer. They'll know by now that their most powerful ally's been dismembered, literally and figuratively. They'll run and hide when it's clear that there's no hope. Only their arrogance has kept them in place for as long as it has. If they lose their second ally, we might never see them again, and I prefer not to leave any loose ends. A couple of them are grudge-holders. They're powerful men with the means to disappear for years."

"But isn't that their weakness too?" Millicent rarely spoke at these meetings, but I was glad she was talking now, giving another perspective. "They can't hobnob and show off. They can't go to the opera or to dinner at the latest and greatest restaurant. They also can't be involved in government meetings." Our enemies had weaknesses, and it was hopefully what would bring them down. Ego with a side of psychopath. They likely couldn't believe we could beat them, and they probably trusted their high-up contacts would keep them safe.

Angelica inclined her head. "Yes, you're right. And we have to rely on this and their indignation to keep them within our reach until tomorrow. I daresay they still think they're somehow going to come out on top."

Prentice cleared his throat. "Well, on that front, I have news." Angelica's hint of raised eyebrows was quickly smothered under a poker face. Hmm, something she didn't know. Ha. It was nice not to be the only one who was last to know. "I heard from Lord Alvin." Ooh, I liked the lord already since he had a chipmunk name, and chipmunks were a kind of squirrel. Oh my God, chipmunks! I needed one. But they weren't over here. Maybe I should visit America so I could meet some. I reached into my pocket to get my phone and google them, but then I remembered where I was. Sighing, I slid it back in. Stupid meetings. "He's attending a soiree at 10 Downing Street. Apparently, the prime minister is in their pocket. They have something on him and have said if they're arrested, they've made it so the information is released. It would mean the end of the PM's career and possibly even gaol time. It would be a PR disaster for this country."

Angelica stared at Prentice for a moment, her mouth pressed into a thin line. "Do you know where they're keeping that information? Do you even know what that information is?"

He adjusted his tie and swallowed. "We don't know where the information is being kept."

Angelica raised one eyebrow. "So you know what it is."

He cleared his throat. "Yes, but I'm not at liberty to divulge that here and now. I'm happy to meet with you after this, Agent DuPree."

She gave a nod. "Good. Right." She took a deep breath. "Give me a moment." She stared at the table, thinking. Well, looked like the directors had covered a lot of bases, but if anyone could come up with a plan, Angelica could. She stood. "If you would accompany me to my office, I want to sort this out immediately. Then I'm going downstairs to talk to one of our captives." She turned her gaze to me. "Lily, I have a feeling that we're going to need your services this afternoon and tomorrow when that soiree is on, and you'll need to know what we're looking for. You'll find out anyway if you hit on it, and if you don't, we're going to have to suffer the directors and their murderous ways for a long time. Tomorrow will be the perfect opportunity to search their abodes because they'll be out."

Prentice stood. "She'll have to sign a special NDA."

I shrugged. "I'll sign whatever you want. I don't care about gossiping about the PM, and I certainly don't care about him as a person. Politicians aren't my favourite people in the world. He's not even my PM." I shrugged.

Imani smirked. "So, Lily, tell me because I'm not sure—do you care about our PM?"

Liv snorted, and Beren grinned. I answered with a smile.

"Right. Come on, then." Angelica looked at me as she and Prentice crossed the room to the door. "The rest of you, please wait for us to return."

I followed them to Angelica's office. She shut the door to

the outer office and made a bubble of silence. Her magic tingled my scalp again, and an NDA appeared. "Sign this, dear." She handed me a pen from the container on her desk. I read some of the first page just to make sure it was an NDA—not that she'd try to fool me with this, but it was a good habit to be in, not signing stuff you had no idea about. I signed it, and she handed it to Prentice. "Now, what's this all about?"

He met Angelica's gaze with a serious one that held reluctance and then, finally, acceptance—we didn't have all day. "Our PM sold British and American defence secrets to a Russian diplomat. We weren't sure how to handle it, so we sat on it. The last thing we need is an unstable government—a few of his ministers knew of it and did nothing. We approached him and suggested he didn't do that again."

"So a threat without a threat."

"Yes, and he stopped, the US none the wiser. His term is over soon, and he's agreed not to run again. But if the public gets wind of this, not only will our people lose total faith in the government, but it will set our relationship with the US back decades. We can't afford to have bad blood with them. This would be a national disaster."

Kudos to Angelica—she'd retained her poker face through every distressing word. "Yes, I see. But there's more?"

He loosened his tie. "Yes. Because one of the ministers involved was a witch, we felt the directors of the PIB should know. We're the ones who told them. They've done some digging of their own and have photos of the information exchange and an admission from the Russian diplomat."

My eyes widened. "Is the diplomat a witch?"

Prentice shrugged. "I have no idea."

"You can give me the diplomat's details, and I'll find out. In any case"—Angelica looked at Prentice—"whether the directors used force or a large bribe to get him to talk, the result is the same." Yikes. MI6 was supposed to protect England, not aid in its downfall. What a disaster.

"Yes, unfortunately. And now we have them blackmailing the prime minister." He sighed. "I'm sorry, Agent DuPree. Our judgement was way off."

She allowed a dash of sympathy to show in her expression. "You followed protocol. You weren't to know what the directors were planning. I've been fighting them from the shadows for the past two years, slowly putting things into place, but they moved faster than I anticipated, and we've been trying to catch up. You're not the only one who was caught short." She wandered to the other side of her desk and placed her hands on the top of her chair. "So, we must forget what's gone and focus on what's to come. Here's what we're going to do."

CHAPTER 14

After talking to Chadiot, Angelica had reached the conclusion that the information we sought was either at the home of Director Brosnan or Director Moore. They were the two more controlling ones, and they wouldn't have trusted the others to keep the information safe until they wanted to use it. She'd also used Chadiot's body language to come to her assumptions. He couldn't say anything outright without dying, so she had to work around that.

My squirrels had been called into action again. The evening light was fading as Grey the Brave sat on the windowsill of Director Brosnan's townhouse, spying on him with his little camera in place. We also had Agent Plover on security at Number 10 Downing Street. She was going to confirm by text when the directors were all there. We didn't want any surprises.

Angelica, Imani, Will, and I sat in a café a block away, watching the live feed on Angelica's phone from GTB. I crossed my fingers that we would find the documents and be able to call it a night, well, apart from the arresting-the-directors thing that would follow our success at recovering those documents. If we didn't find what we needed, we were onto the next director's house, and then the next, etcetera.

Please don't come to that.

In the meantime, the rest of our crew waited in a PIB flat a street away from the PM's place. Once we, hopefully, recovered the documents, we were meeting them there, and then our arrest process would begin. It wasn't going to be easy because most of the soiree attendees weren't witches and didn't know about them. There was also press there covering the event.

Yep, just another day working for the PIB.

But we were so close to the finish line. So close to Will and me getting married. Did I dare hope this war would soon be over? My gaze travelled from the boring screen, where nothing much was happening, to Will's gorgeous face. I resisted the urge to reach across and run my fingers over the stubble covering his sharp jawline. His brooding blue eyes turned my way. When he looked at me with heat in his eyes, my stomach still did little flips. Then he smiled, and I couldn't help but return it. He'd brought me so much love and joy. Surely, we deserved our happy ending.

"Ah, there. He's just left." Angelica's look of satisfaction was aimed at the phone. She looked up. "We'll wait for Agent Plover's confirmation; then we move."

I bit my fingernail, and Imani slapped it out of my mouth. "Stop that! So gross."

"Hey, it's my coping mechanism. Do you want me to freak out?" Okay, so I was exaggerating, but every time she did that, it irritated the heck out of me.

"Do you know how many germs are on your hands and in your mouth? Now they're combined, you'll touch things, and everyone else will be exposed to your super germs." She shuddered.

I chuckled and reached towards her face, waggling my fingers. "Watch out for my fingertips of death. The germs are coming. Mwahahahahaha!" She leaned away, eyes bugging out, and almost fell off her chair.

Angelica's phone dinged. She looked at the message, gave a nod to Will, and stood. She stared down at Imani and me. "Okay, children, it's time to go. Do I need to change your nappies before we leave?" We both snorted. Will bit back a smile, and Angelica rolled her eyes. "I can't believe I'm trusting you to save lives." She shook her head as she left the café.

Imani shoved me, and I shoved her back as we walked down the street. At least she was helping me dissipate my nervous energy in a way that was more acceptable to her. Will stayed a pace behind us, amusement on his face.

All too soon, we were within sight of Brosnan's white, three-storey terrace house. Angelica, Imani, and I stopped. Will's magic tingled my scalp, and he pulled out a pair of dark sunglasses and a baseball cap from his inside jacket pocket and put them on. The disguise worked because he wasn't wearing his suit. Angelica had us all wearing jeans and casual tops, but we were all in black. Maybe we looked weird, or maybe we looked like bar staff walking to work.

Will moved closer to the property while we waited. Grey the Brave must've been watching for us. As soon as Will got near the property, the squirrel came racing through the iron-bar front fence and straight for me. He scrambled up my leg. I laughed. "Hello, cutie. You did a great job. Thank you." I pulled a nut out of my pocket and gave it to him.

Will smiled but then turned his back on us, probably because he needed to concentrate. As usual, it was his job to disable the security cameras and alarm, both magical and non-magical. It took him eight minutes before he waved us over.

We all followed him up the three steps to the front door, which he opened easily and walked in. Adrenaline warmed my chest. A shiver scurried down my spine, and I glanced around to make sure we weren't being watched. How was that so easy? Was it a trap? "Ma'am, are we going to get ambushed? That seemed too easy." Will gave me an insulted look. "Sorry. I didn't mean you weren't good at disarming security things. It's just…." Foot meet mouth.

Angelica shared a sly look with Will and said, "They used to get the best in the PIB to oversee their security each year. Guess who that happened to be?" Will bowed with a hand flourish.

Imani laughed. "And they were too stupid to change things after they waged war on us?"

"They most likely didn't think. Besides, they needed good security against the mafia more than against us, and Will is the best." Angelica gazed at him as if he were her favourite child. She looked back at me. "Now, dear, you know what you have to do. The rest of us will search for evidence in the here and now and keep an eye out, and Grey the Brave can patrol out the front."

"Okay." I took my phone from my pocket and brought up the photo app. "Show me any of the directors putting away the evidence of the current prime minister's treason." That should be specific enough. I also pictured the prime minister in my head and ambled down the hallway, then from one palatial room to the next. From original oil paintings in massive gilt frames to Persian rugs and crystal chandeliers, this guy was flaunting the money.

I wandered around, not finding anything until I got to the study. Brosnan was in here by himself. The documents and a few pictures were spread out on his desk. Yes! Satisfaction spread through me. I loved when my talent worked. Even though I hadn't had any problems, you never knew when something would just stop. Maybe I'd have as much faith in it one day as everyone else seemed to have in me.

He stood staring down at them with his arms folded, a grin in place around a big, fat cigar. I could almost smell the sweet smoke. I took a photo from the doorway to get the whole scene in; then I walked to the table to see what was splayed on its surface.

Pictures of the prime minister handing a folder to a middle-aged man in an expensive suit. The man had blond hair and high, sharp cheekbones. A gun sat on the table between them. Another picture showed the prime minister looking on while the Russian perused at plans for something, a weapon maybe. Another photo showed the Russian reading something that had a logo for the Ministry of Defence on the top. I wasn't going to stop to read it—Angelica could figure it out later. Anyway, MI6 had the same information. I took another photo, then left it. We needed to know where the stuff was now. My magic was supposed to show him putting it away or the moment just before. Hmm. I'd have to try again.

"Show Brosnan putting the documents away." I frowned. He wasn't in here. Maybe he figured this place was too obvious. I went to the kitchen—the last room on this floor I hadn't seen. Nope. Up to the first floor. Nothing. One floor to go.

The top floor had two bedrooms and a bathroom. The

bedrooms were clear. I sighed. The bathroom wasn't likely to be the hiding place, but it was the last room left. I entered the white-tiled space. A black single vanity with a white marble top sat under an oval mirror. Black taps and accents provided a pleasant contrast. The guy had good taste—I had to give him that.

I asked my magic again to show him putting the documents away, and there he was. Oh, it was playing as a video. I switched to that and pressed Record. Brosnan stood at the vanity, the two-inch-thick pile of documents in his arms. He turned on one vanity tap and then the other. Was he going to destroy them? That didn't make sense. My brow tightened. So weird.

He went to the freestanding bath and turned on both those taps, then the shower. Water gushed out of the rainwater showerhead. Now what? He flushed the toilet. Of course he did. That made total sense. Did he have some kind of OCD?

Oh. When the toilet flushed, a four-foot by four-foot square of tiles lifted a few inches from the floor. He slid the documents into the shallow cubbyhole, then turned off all the taps. Once he'd done that, he flushed the toilet, and the tile lid lowered, sliding perfectly back in place so that there was no way you could tell it was a secret hiding place. Hmm, nifty but kind of dramatic. Surely there could've been an easier way to open it. He dusted his hands together and walked out. My video stopped.

I went to the top of the stairs and called, "I think I found it." I didn't want to uncover it without everyone watching. If we ever needed to corroborate where we found it and that I didn't plant anything, I'd need witnesses, plus I was sure Angelica wanted to watch this, if for no other reason than it was elaborate.

Will and Angelica came upstairs. "Where's Imani?"

"I've left her on watch, dear. So, show me."

"Right, it's a bit weird, so bear with me." I wasn't even sure if it was going to work. I was pretty sure his magic would've shown up on the screen if he'd used any. But what if it didn't, and it was booby-trapped?

"Lily, what are you waiting for?" Will stared at me.

"Oh, um, I don't think there's a spell on it, but can you check for booby traps?"

"Okay." Will's magic caressed my nape. He whispered a few words. "There's an alarm in this room. Interesting."

My eyes widened, and I looked at the doorway and into the hallway. "Does he know we're in here?" My heart raced, and I threw up my return to sender.

Will shook his head. "No. It's only on the hiding place, which is just there." He pointed to the area I'd seen elevate. "Just a moment." He did his thing, and after a couple of minutes, he smiled. "Disarmed."

I blew out a rushed breath and placed a hand on my thudding heart. "Okay, phew."

"Can we get on with it now, dear?" Hmm, not thanks for making sure we weren't discovered. Sheesh.

"Yes, Ma'am." I turned on all the taps in the order I'd seen him do it. I held my breath as my finger hovered over the toilet button. Will and Angelica were looking at me as if I'd lost the plot, but maybe that was more for whatever ritual Brosnan had set up. I flushed. *Please work.*

The tiles lifted. Yes! I couldn't help but state the obvious. "There it is. The documents should be in there."

Will knelt on the floor and reached in. He pulled out what looked like more than I'd seen Brosnan put in there. He stood and opened them, allowing Angelica to observe as he leafed through everything. "Yep, looks like these are the pictures and proof." He kept going through them. "Oh, what's this?"

Angelica's mouth opened a fraction, revealing as much surprise as she ever would. She grabbed a few pieces of paper and read. After a minute of skimming, she looked at Will. "This is one of the agreements signed by Cozzolino. I'm assuming the other documents are here too. And this page is an order to terminate MI6 agents signed by all three crime families." She smiled. "We've got them!" I grinned, and so did Will. She turned to me. "Well done, Lily. Well done." Her magic vibrated against my scalp. "Are there any copies of these?" She stared at the pages. A blue aura surrounded them. After a few seconds, it changed to red. "No, good." She magicked them away, probably to her super-secret-squirrel location, where she kept all the really important stuff. "Let's get Imani and Grey the Brave and head to Number Ten. This ends tonight."

⬥

We came out in the bathroom of the PIB safe house near the prime minister's residence. Beren, Millicent, Lavender, and Sarah waited for us. James was heading up the takedown of criminal syndicate number two. They were located around the UK in various locations. Angelica had timed it so that we'd go after them simultaneously. The third group, being the easiest, we could clean up over the next few days. We'd spread ourselves thin as it was.

Angelica looked at Will, Imani, and me. "Uniforms, please. And, Lily, Grey can go back to HQ."

"How's he supposed to press the intercom?" There was nothing for him to climb up to the pad on the wall, and there was no way he could jump and press the button before falling to the ground.

She rolled her eyes. "Take him there, for goodness' sake, and come straight back."

"Yes, Ma'am." Everyone stared at me as I made my doorway and scooted through. I gave GTB a kiss on the head and handed him off to Gus with instructions to let him outside. I magicked my uniform on while I was in the PIB reception room and magicked my new handcuffs to myself, then made a doorway back to the safe house. Angelica had kindly given me another pair last night.

Angelica stood at one end of the apartment's living room. Everyone faced her in a semicircle. "Right, now Lily's back, we can continue." Again everyone turned to me. Imani smirked, and Beren winked. I shrugged. Surely Angelica should be used to me by now. Besides, she was the one who kept asking me to attend these things. She got what she got. "Agent Bianchi"— she was looking at Millicent—"you're going to cast and hold the no-leave spell on the building. I'm afraid that will take most of your attention, so I want you safely outside."

"Yes, Ma'am." I was glad Angelica was keeping her safer than us. James was in a dangerous situation, no doubt, and they couldn't leave my niece an orphan. A reminder of why having kids was a bad idea. I wanted to ditch the PIB, but now I was contracted to MI6 for a year, even if we won today, I had commitments for at least twelve months, and Will wasn't ever quitting the PIB. If we had kids and something happened to him…. There was no way I could do it alone.

"Everyone else, I'm assigning each person to a certain director. It's your job to contain and arrest them. I'll try not to get involved because if things get out of hand, I'll have memory wipes to do, and I'll also have to make sure no one videos any witch activity and posts it on the internet. The press is there, and while photographs could be seen as fakes, videos are harder to fake, and if more than one is taken and posted, we'll have a hell of a time trying to get them off before it causes trouble. We're not going to time this—we're going in and getting it done as quickly as possible." Her gaze roved the group. "When you've finished arresting your director, you'll have to guard them until we're done because of the no-leave spell." She gave everyone their assigned directors. Imani and I got Brosnan. He was the most powerful director. I wanted to tell her to put Will on it rather than me, but she had a reason for her decision, so I kept my mouth shut.

"We're going in the front door today. I have no doubt that they'll be watching the reception room to see who comes out. I want as much surprise on our side as possible. Once we're in, Agent Bianchi can cast the no-leave spell. So, are we ready?"

I took a deep breath, my heart racing and a funny feeling lodged in my throat. Imani whispered, "We've got this, Lily." She held her hand up for a fist bump. I obliged.

"Okay, no-notice spells on. Let's do this." Angelica strode out the front door full of confidence. How did she really feel? What were our chances of beating them? They must've anticipated this was coming at some point. There was little chance they would guess it was happening at such an obvious place. I crossed my fingers that surprise really was on our side.

Our group of suited-up agents didn't get any stares as we made our way to Number Ten. Thank you, magic. If we'd been normal, there's no way people wouldn't have stared at Beren and Will, two of the hottest men ever, and put them in black suits, and well, they stood out. Imani cut a gorgeous and imposing figure in her suit too. A tall, stunning woman with flawless dark skin who looked like she had ninja skills. Even

Angelica had an aura about her. The way she moved was more like a thirty-year-old than a middle-aged woman. I basked in their glow to fortify my confidence.

We had this.

When we reached the high iron gates, Angelica said a few words to the police guards manning the checkpoint and showed them ID. I wasn't sure if she knew them, if we were given prior approval, or if she used her talent, but within a minute, they were nodding and ushering us through. One of the police escorted us to the drab, dark, four-storey brick building and knocked on the black front door. A butler opened it. As I overtook Millicent on my way to the door, I said, "Good luck."

"You too."

I dropped my no-notice and put up my return to sender and shield. As soon as the directors saw us, they'd know. We went through a bland-looking entrance room with a black-and-white checkered floor. We passed two men in suits going downstairs as we ascended the grand staircase. They weren't witches, and their gazes followed us.

We were in a hurry, so I only briefly noticed the large portraits lining the walls around the staircase. The decorations were classic ye olde England—plush, elegant, and expensive-looking.

Angelica led us down a corridor with a couple of turns. This place was a rabbit warren. Three wait staff hurried past with empty trays. The murmur of voices and laughter and clinking of glasses floated through the hallway. We cut through some kind of dining room into a large, high-ceilinged drawing room filled with people in cocktail attire. Again, huge oil paintings crowded the walls. I was sure I'd seen a couple of them before, at least online. This artwork would be worth a fortune.

A massive cream-coloured Persian rug covered most of the herringbone timber floor. Hovering over the middle of the room was a grand chandelier, and two wide ionic columns at one end of the room dominated it.

If things came to magical blows and we destroyed some of this, would it be fixable? If not, I didn't know how they would explain it on the insurance form. Best not to think about that. I shook my head. Time to look for our quarry in the crowd.

Imani and I stuck together. The doors were open on the other side of the room, and I saw Will and Beren enter. So there were even more people. This could get messy.

A few of the crowd turned and stared at us. One woman even made a face at our—I'm assuming from her sour look— terrible fashion choices. She "whispered" to her friend loud enough for us to hear, "Who invited those uncouth women? Dressing like men. Honestly. Must be feminists." She rolled her eyes and took a sip of champagne. Argh, some people were the worst. Feminists were awesome, and funnily enough, I was one. I didn't see the insult.

I was about to retort with a witty comeback when I stilled. The crowd had parted, revealing Brosnan standing a few feet away. How I could've missed him was beyond me since he wore his stupid top hat. I hoped Will had just as much luck finding Director Moore.

I whispered, "He's over there, talking to an older woman in a red dress."

Imani gazed at where I'd given a subtle nod. Her eyes widened. "He's not even wearing any protection spells. Either he's arrogant as all hell, or he's an idiot."

"I'm betting the first one. He almost managed to destroy the PIB. I'm thinking his IQ is okay. So, how are we going to do this? Do you want me to distract him while you cuff him?"

She smiled. "Sounds good to me."

I shuffled my way through the prime minister's well-to-do guests. Just before I reached Brosnan, he looked at me and smiled. There was no surprise in his gaze. Crap. "Ah, good afternoon. Miss Bianchi, isn't it?" His hands cradled his wine glass.

"Hello, Mr Brosnan." I wasn't going to call him a director. As far as the new PIB was concerned, it had no directors.

"Are you going to introduce me to your friend?" the woman asked. Her brown hair was arranged in an elegant chignon, and she patted it and smiled.

"Ah, yes. Marisol Bowen-Thorpe, please meet Lily Bianchi. An acquaintance. Her brother and fiancé used to work for me."

Imani was a few feet away behind the group of people standing behind Brosnan. She was likely waiting for him to put his hands by his sides. He'd also put his protection spells up. So, he *was* worried. He probably hadn't been expecting us at such a public place. I avoided looking at her, just in case he hadn't noticed. Instead, I smiled at Marisol Bowen-Thorpe. "Lovely to meet you."

"Likewise."

Imani had moved closer. Maybe I could facilitate things by grabbing one of his wrists. If I did that, he'd be pulling his arms back, and I could let go and he'd fling back into Imani. It was worth a try.

"If you ladies would excuse me, I need to, ahem, use the little boy's room."

"Of course, darling." Marisol batted her lashes at him.

"What? Leaving so soon? I don't think so."

He plastered on a fake smile. "I'm not sure what you mean. Are you trying to embarrass me?"

Marisol's forehead wrinkled as her gaze darted between us. I smiled. "Of course not, but if you think you're leaving, I'm afraid no one's coming in or out at the moment. They've added security."

A storm gathered in his face. I was about to grab his wrist, now that Imani was behind him, but shouting came from the other reception room. Magic tingled my scalp. Crap.

The crowd hushed and turned towards the commotion. Glass crashed, and someone shouted, "No!"

Red wine sloshed in my face, the sharp scent of it drenching my nostrils. I blinked to clear my eyes.

Brosnan had thrown his wine in my face and had turned to run… straight into Imani's waiting arms. I smiled as she clicked the handcuffs on one wrist. He was wrestling with her to save his other wrist. She was strong, but maybe not strong enough to gain control of a panicked man. I did the first thing that came to mind, and I tickled him. It was ridiculous but effective. Imani was so close to putting his wrists close together.

At the last second, he dropped his protection spell. His magic zinged my scalp, and a chair materialised in the air above Imani's head and dropped on her. It bounced off her shield, thank God. But then a large porcelain lamp appeared.

The crowd stared. A loud thud came from the other room, and someone screamed. Yikes. In my peripheral, photographers took pictures or videos or whatever. This wasn't good. But then Angelica was there, her magic sparking over my nape. Photographers were looking at their cameras and shaking them as if something was wrong. Phew.

But Brosnan wasn't done, and if I hadn't seen it, I wouldn't have believed it. A baby grand piano appeared in the air above Imani. I tried to scream at her to watch out, but there was no time. It fell heavily, throwing Imani to the floor. Shields had their limit, unfortunately. With his way cleared, he jumped around the piano and ran for the door. I dropped to the floor. *Oh my God, please be okay.* Imani was dazed, but she held her thumb up. The air rushed out of me. She was alive. "Are you all right for a minute?"

"Go after him. Go." Her voice was low and pained. Two of the legs had broken when it landed, so there was a gap she could crawl out of. I didn't want to leave her, but if Brosnan got away, we might never find him. Ever. "I'll be back in a minute." I jumped up and yelled at the men watching, "Get her out from under there. Now!" They snapped out of the shock they were in and sprung to action. Others were staring at the door we'd come in earlier, so I sprinted in that direction, pushing people out of my way.

Through the dining room, then into the hall. I ran to the first turn. Agent Plover stood in Brosnan's way, her gun trained on him. "Don't move or I'll shoot."

He threw his shield up and walked towards her. She spied me over his shoulder. He stopped and turned. "Ah, Lily, we meet again."

"You sound like you've been to villain school." What was I going to do? How could I trap him when he dropped pianos on people? Maybe he was weaker after translocating those things? I glanced up. At least the hallway was smaller. He could possibly drop another chair, or a garden pot. Hmm, that would hurt.

Agent Plover's gun was still trained on him. "Put your hands behind your back, or I'll shoot."

He laughed. I knew her shots wouldn't do much, but maybe they would weaken him enough or distract him so I could slap the cuffs on. Wasn't Angelica worried I could've been shot in the head yesterday? Hmm. "Take your shot.

Shoot him, Plover. Make it a few times." She looked at me as if I'd just eaten poo. "Just do it!"

Her gun went off twice, the bullets bouncing off his shield, but I saw the wince. He was weakening. He ran to her, copped one more bullet but punched her in the face. She staggered back. He grabbed her and stood behind her, putting her in a chokehold. "I'll kill her if you don't let me go."

Agent Plover held his arm with both hands, trying to drag it down off her throat. "Don't listen to him. Do what you have to."

If only I had a gun or something. I guess I could do what he'd done—throw things at him. I looked around. A blue-and-white vase sat on a table. I hoped it wasn't a rare antique. Here went nothing. I picked it up and advanced on him. He kept Plover in front of him as he backed along the corridor.

Imani wasn't here yet. Was she okay? How badly was she hurt? *Stop, Lily. Concentrate.* As much as I cared about Imani, I couldn't let him get away. If only there was some way to tell Angelica to check on her. Imani couldn't even make a doorway to get back to HQ. Crap.

Magic scraped along my skull. It wasn't anyone I knew, and it wasn't Brosnan. More screams came from the reception rooms, gunshots, glass smashing. What a disaster this had turned into, and the press were taking it all in. If our secret wasn't out after this, it would be a bloody miracle.

I sensed something above me and dove forward and rolled. I had to drop the vase, and it clunked to the carpet. Thank you to whoever covered the timber floors. A dull thud came from where I'd been standing. A small armchair. Holy crap. That would've hurt. Anger surged through me, and I stared him down as he dragged Plover backwards towards the stairs, his shield back up.

I was done playing.

I grabbed the vase and ran for him. He tried to keep Plover in front of me. She handed me the gun. Yikes. I had no idea how to use it. Was it ready to shoot? There was only one way to find out. I jogged to keep up with them and pointed the gun at his head, but he kept pushing Plover in my way. I aimed the gun at the ceiling—it was too dangerous.

My breath came fast, and my heart galloped. Plover threw her gaze to the side and mouthed, "On three." She held up one finger at a time. One, two… three! I dropped my shield. She jerked her head to the side, and I braced myself and shot once. The gun discharged, the force of it surprising. It was a direct hit in Brosnan's face. His shield held, but he winced. Finally, I was getting somewhere. I put my shield back up.

We'd reached the stairs. I flicked my gaze up. Nothing yet. I could try to lightning bolt him, but if his return to sender was as strong as mine, I'd just about kill myself. I'd shoot him again, but I didn't know if there were any bullets left, and I didn't want to hit Plover. Hmm. Actually….

I drew my magic, dropped my shield, and threw a shield around her, then raised the gun, dodged to the side, and shot Brosnan in the head again. His shield wavered. He would've felt that. His answer was to move his grip to Plover's upper arms, turn her, and push her down the stairs.

Crap.

My shield was buffeted as she fell, each knock and thump like a small fist in my stomach. She should be okay, maybe bruised, but I couldn't afford to take my gaze from Brosnan. I held the gun to his face and pulled the trigger.

Nothing.

I swore. And I never swore.

Brosnan swung for my face. I dodged out of the way and

tried to kick him in the shin. This was ridiculous. I could try and shove him down the stairs, but he might grab me and take me with him. If only I carried a knife. How was everyone else doing? I shoved that thought away—not constructive—and put my shield back up.

"You, young girlie, are not going to take me away. You're nothing compared to me." He tried to make a doorway, but it wouldn't form. I'd like to make a doorway and cut him in half. Damn that I couldn't.

Then it hit me. I couldn't push him down the stairs with my hands. There would be a push back, but I had to try it.

He ran at me and landed a punch to my face. My head jerked back, but all I felt was a nudge. Rage ignited in his gaze, his fists flying faster. I staggered back and fell on the floor. This was ridiculous. I was supposed to be a powerful witch, and I was cowering on the ground?

Then I remembered a move James had taught me years ago. I shoved my shoulders against his shins, gripped his heels with my hands, and leaned forward with force. He fell on his backside. I leapt up.

The armchair he'd tried to drop on me was lying in the hallway. Hatred fused my grin with something that probably didn't look sane. He scrambled to get up.

"Thanks for the brilliant idea." I dropped my shield again.

His confused face paled when he saw that I'd translocated the armchair to the ceiling above his head. It dropped on him. His shield shattered, and he crumpled to the ground.

His arms were sticking out, Imani's handcuff still hanging from one wrist. I picked the other side of the cuff up and closed it over the other wrist, then felt for a pulse. He was still alive, more's the shame. I didn't want to leave him, so I awkwardly shifted the armchair off him. Maybe I could take him outside and move him to HQ.

I rolled him onto his back and grabbed his arms. He was heavy, but I managed to grip his wrists and drag him down the stairs, his legs making a satisfying thud as they bumped down each stair. A waiter stood at the bottom of the stairs staring up at Plover. "Can you see if she's okay?" I asked. He gazed at me because, hell, I didn't look weird dragging a handcuffed man down the stairs. "Please? She's hurt. She might need an ambulance." I would've suggested Beren look at her, but he'd have his hands full if the sounds of fighting were anything to go by. What if he or Will were hurt? The waiter finally did the right thing and went up to her.

I blew out a harried breath and hauled Brosnan to the front door. I won't lie—I had to stop three times for a break. Dragging people was hard work.

I opened the door—all the staff seemed to have disappeared—and called to Millicent. Her brow furrowed as she stood staring at the building, sweat glistening on her forehead. "I need to come out and make a doorway to get rid of him."

"I can't drop the spell, Lily. I've just had another attempt to leave."

I sighed. "Fine. I'll think of something else. Also, do you need help?"

"No, I'll hold. But can you just go and make sure they finish soon? I've probably only got fifteen minutes left in me." Dark circles stained the skin under her eyes.

"Will do." I shut the front door. He was handcuffed but starting to come around. It would drain me, but I needed to be sure. I cast a freeze spell on him. "I'll be back soon."

When I reached the stairs, the waiter was giving Agent

Plover a drink of water. She was sitting with her back against the wall. "Are you okay?"

"Yes. Thank you. Whatever you did, it saved my life."

"I wouldn't go that far, but I at least saved you a few more bruises. I have to go up now, but I'm dropping your shield. Brosnan's been neutralised." And I needed all the energy I could get.

Her mouth dropped open. "You killed him?"

"Ah, no. He's just handcuffed and… ah… frozen." I couldn't say too much in front of the waiter, even though he'd probably seen his fill of weirdly impossible today. "I'll be back."

I sprinted up the stairs, two at a time. The crowd had moved to the outer edges of the room, a few of them sitting on chairs staring at each other in shock, their faces pale, eyes haunted. Angelica wasn't here, and neither was Imani. My stomach somersaulted. What had happened?

I wanted to run to the next room, but I'd sneak. Hugging as close to the wall as I could, I made my way to the doorway and crouched out of the immediate line of sight of anyone standing.

I peered around the doorway. To my left, Beren was lying on the floor in the corner, Imani kneeling next to him, her magic glowing. My breath caught in my throat. Not B. I blinked, trying my best not to cry. Now wasn't the time. Imani didn't even notice me—her magic was pouring into Beren, and she wore a return to sender.

My gaze travelled the room. Two of the directors lay on the floor, unmoving, one of them with staring eyes and blood coming out of his nose. Will, Lavender, Angelica, and Sarah faced the other two directors who stood with four witches at the other end of the room. They were part of the second criminal group. Two large men, one bald, one with a mullet and facial tattoos, and two women, both with long brown hair, one slim, the other muscled and sporting a nose ring. I couldn't forget seeing them in the paperwork Angelica had given us.

There were no civilians in this room—they'd wisely found somewhere else to be. With the no-leave spell, they couldn't actually flee the home. Maybe they were holed up in a bedroom somewhere because the crowd in the reception room was a third of what it had been.

The witches were taking turns hurling fire, then electrical bolts. One side would lower their shield, then shoot, quickly putting the shield back up for the bounce back of the return to sender. They were betting on who would fail first. What a mess.

A lightning bolt speared down, cracking onto Will's shield. It looked as if two of them each held a shield. Had they gone through two shields already? I studied their auras. Will and Angelica were still strong, but Lavender and Sarah were fading. Sarah swayed, and Will grabbed her with a steadying hand. Four against six wasn't an even battle.

Luckily, I was here.

I smiled. This ended soon.

As the enemy's shield closed, Angelica and Will dropped theirs, and Will called up a fireball. It speared across the room and slammed into the directors' shield, the flames curling around it and dissipating harmlessly. Their auras were fading, too, but they had more energy left collectively than my friends.

I had to get my timing right. I sat back behind the wall, out of sight. If they saw me glowing, my advantage would be lost. Sweat trickled down my forehead. I swallowed my fear. My gaze swept the room one more time for any enemies, and I dropped my protection spells. I needed all the energy I could get.

My stomach ached as I opened myself up to as much power as I could hold. Heat radiated off my skin. My mouth was so dry. What I wouldn't give for a cold drink.

Another crack sounded, and Sarah cried out.

No!

Images of Imani pinned under the piano, Beren on the floor—was he even alive—filled my mind. Fury sizzled under my skin, melding with my power.

I popped my head back around and waited for my moment.

I mouthed the spell to call down lightning. They would drop their shield any moment.

Adrenaline flooded my stomach as I waited. I forced my shallow breaths to lengthen before I passed out. It was like being at the starting line, waiting for the gun to go off. I clenched my fists. Stopped breathing.

They dropped their shield, and before they could call down their spell, I released my magic.

Thunder decimated the silence as a blinding flash of white-hot light speared the ceiling. It directly hit one of the men and one of the women criminals and exploded outwards, scalding blades of electricity shooting into the rest of the group.

The two who'd taken the direct hit were pulverised to ash. The other woman had a hole in her stomach that no one could survive. The directors and their last ally lay groaning on the floor, blisters and red-raw skin revealed from the holes rent in their clothing.

Angelica looked at me, her mouth falling open. She closed it, her expression grateful, relieved, exhausted. Her nod said thank you. She flicked her gaze to Beren and Imani, and I knew what she asked. Then she, Will, Lavender, and Sarah hurried to cuff the remaining enemies.

I ran to Imani and Beren. "Is he…?" The last word died in my throat, and I pretended my eyes weren't burning with unshed tears.

Imani's frantic eyes met mine. "No. He's still alive, but barely. He took a massive blow to the head."

I pulled my phone out and called Millicent. "Take the shield off now. We won. We've got them all, but Beren's badly hurt. We have to get him to headquarters, ASAP. Also, can you deal with that douche I left in the doorway? Thank you."

"Will do. You're free to go. I'll see you soon. Bye." Thank God Millicent was still okay.

I slid my phone back into my pocket.

Imani's eyebrows raised. "*Language*, Lily."

I shrugged. On the scale of rude words, douche wasn't *that* bad, and it seemed highly appropriate in the moment. "I'm going to make the doorway around us. Stay still." I made my doorway, uncaring that people were watching. Let them watch. I had a friend to save.

It took five more days to finish arresting all the other players, and we'd lost two agents doing it. Finally, everyone who needed to be in gaol was there. It was a sombre meeting in the conference room. Agents Plover and Prentice attended, as did Phillip. He sat next to Angelica. He touched her hand or thigh every now and then, which earned him small smiles and, God forbid, loving gazes. Funnily enough, she cut those off when she started the meeting.

She only had to assume her poker face and stare down the table, and everyone went quiet. "The hard work is over... for now." She hadn't called us in just for that. "Thank you all for your dedication and commitment to seeing this through. It's been a long time coming, something I've been fighting against for a considerable amount of time. From now on, we must remain vigilant. There might be one or two seeds that have flown from our grasp. We don't want them to take root."

I sighed and slumped a little. Honestly, would this ever be over? Angelica had managed to contain the reporters and mind wipe them and the others who'd seen what had happened. It was a massive job. MI6 had helped us get everything off the internet as well. But as far as full-on enemies were concerned, surely we weren't about to face a similar threat. We'd downed the biggest players. Will grabbed my hand and held it. I gave him a grateful smile.

Angelica sat up straighter. "That's just a reminder, so don't worry. For now, it's back to business as usual… almost. As you all know, we're now in partnership with MI6, which means our assignments will be mixed with theirs. I know everyone needs a break, but it's going to have to wait a few months while we ensure the integration of our two agent communities. We'll all be learning from each other. When we're working on MI6 cases, we follow their protocols, and you'll take orders from them. When they're here, it's vice versa. It will require extra training. And remember, we need to be discreet when dealing with non-witch crime. Any questions?"

I wasn't a spoiled child, but what the hell? I shut my eyes. Maybe there would never be a good time for Will and me to get married. So much for visiting Australia soon. Maybe Will would settle for a long weekend in Spain or something. I guessed we'd be together whether we were married or not. The threat of tears had abated, so I opened my eyes. I was an adult; I could do this.

Will leant into me and whispered in my ear, "Are you okay?"

"Yeah, I will be." I'd had greater disappointments. It's just that I'd held on so long with that as the carrot—we'd all enjoy each other's company, and Will and I would make it official. It would've been good to see my old friends too. Oh well. I took a deep breath and let it go. A bit of disappointment never hurt anyone. Okay, so it did hurt, but it couldn't kill me, could it? At least I had my squirrel army to train. That made me smile. As far as everyone was concerned, the squirrels had been a success, and Angelica wanted to incorporate them into as many cases as she could. They'd helped Beren out with the other criminal groups while we were defeating the directors. It was a relief that they'd been able to take orders from him too.

"So, as much as you've all worked extremely hard the last few months, I need you to go just a bit longer. We'll be recruiting new witches and non-witches with our lovely increased budget." She smiled at Phillip and Prentice. "Life will get easier for us. I promise."

Her phone rang. She frowned and looked at it. "I'm sorry. I have to take this." She answered it. "Agent DuPree speaking. Yes, Agent Link?" She listened for a moment, her poker face going back up. She sighed. "Yes, I'm on it. Thank you." She hung up and stood. "I'm afraid there's been an emergency at Heathrow." She looked at me. "We'll need you, Lily. Someone's called in a bomb threat, and one of the dog handlers is a witch. He said the dogs found no evidence of any bombs, but he's seen a couple of spells. Once you're done, we'll get in our specialist explosives diffusion witches."

They'd put together that team after the potential bomb incident on the Tube. Witches could turn seemingly innocuous materials into explosive devices with the right spells. Millicent's dad was actually working with that department part-time now.

Will's forehead creased. "Make sure you wear your shield."

"Yes, sir." I gave him a mock salute.

"Sorry, I just want you to be safe."

I stood. "Okay. Is anyone coming with me?"

"I'm sending Agent Jawara. You'll meet with Agent Fiddington when you get to our reception room." Who knew the PIB had a reception room at the airport. Interesting. I put up my hand. "Yes, dear."

"Can I have a long weekend to rest?"

She thought for a moment and smiled. "Yes, dear, and I think it's time we moved back into the Westerham property. What do you think?"

My mouth dropped open, and I was surprised by the joy that flowed through me. "Can I even have coffees sitting in Costa?"

"Yes, dear. I think we're safe enough now. Just be watchful."

I looked at the ceiling. "Yes! Finally!"

"So that means I can go home?" Imani asked.

"Yes, dear. It's officially going-back-to-normal day. How does that sound?"

James and Millicent grinned. They were moving in with her parents because their house hadn't been rebuilt yet. They'd decided to look for another one and sell the land as it was.

Well, at least I had something to look forward to... after this job. I turned to Will. "See you at *home*, home."

He smiled. "Stay safe." Worry tightened the edges of his eyes.

"I will."

Imani stood. "Okay, Lily. Let's get this over with."

It was nearing the end of a long day. By the time I'd finished with this, it would be dinner time. The news that we'd be going home pepped me up a bit, and I was surprised to find myself smiling as we walked through Imani's doorway. Imani elbowed me when she came through. "Shield, Lily."

"Ah, crap. Sorry." *Focus.*

Imani buzzed the intercom, and a slim, tall woman with red hair in a sleek bob answered it. "Hi, I'm Agent Fiddington.

You must be Agent Jawara and Agent Bianchi." I was too tired to correct her. Imani just said yes, and I said hello. "Thanks for coming on short notice. We've had to cancel all flights until we can get this sorted. Someone called in the threat, and we saw suspicious activity on our security cameras, but it was interfered with. Witches." She pressed her lips together, totally unimpressed, even though she was a witch. Life would be easier without witch criminals, that was for sure. "Come this way, and keep your eyes and ears open." The reception room opened to a PIB lounge. Nice. I magicked my Nikon to myself before we left the PIB lounge. We hurried through to the public airport area.

I held my camera up and whispered, "Show me someone planting an explosive device here today or yesterday." I wasn't quite sure about the timeline, but I needed to cover my bases.

She led us out a security door into what looked like the baggage sorting area. A Qantas plane sat there. "This plane arrived this morning, and the threat was made just after it landed. We've found evidence of two spells. Before we try and unravel them, we wanted to gather more evidence, just in case something explodes, and it's all destroyed."

I raised my brows. "How likely is it to explode?"

She shrugged. "We're all wearing our protection spells, so we should be okay. But until we sort this out, no flights can come or go from this section. It's going to set us back days."

I looked at Imani. She didn't seem too bothered. Argh, I was so not cut out for this. Just think of the squirrels and the fact that you're going home tonight. I smiled. Yep, things would slowly get back to normal.

"Okay, I'll get to work. Where are the suspicious spells?"

She walked around to the other side of a massive cart of bags. "One of them is just there. Can you see it?"

I looked with my other sight. A glowing red border outlined two bags that sat next to each other. The spell was complicated, and I couldn't follow it properly. "Ah, right. Okay." I asked my magic silently in my head to show me anyone planting an explosive and panned my camera around. I licked my lips, hoping they weren't watching on some camera somewhere, ready to press a button. Shields were not infallible, as I'd recently learned.

Nothing.

I wasn't going to tell her that, though. She wasn't supposed to know my talent. I'd had enough of people being after me to last a lifetime. I took a few photos to throw her off. I gave Imani a look that said I hadn't found anything. She turned to Agent Fiddington. "Was there anything else we needed to look at?"

"Yes. In the galley on the plane. It's a similar spell. The bomb specialists are coming soon, but we need to find who did this before they try it again."

Imani nodded. "Okay, lead the way."

We went back around the wall of bags. Those poor travellers. Were they coming or going? Would they have to sleep on the floor in the airport tonight? Argh, travel really sucked. Maybe it was a good thing we weren't going to Australia yet. Hmm, who knew there could be a silver lining to that. Ha! Put that together with the fact that I'd be sleeping in Westerham tonight, and well, today was actually a good day.

I followed the agent up the portable stairs and into the aircraft. It was eerily empty in economy. We walked through to the galley. I asked my magic again. Nothing. I shook my head at Imani. "Should we check in there?" She nodded at business class.

"Please, go through. I'd rather be thorough now. But be careful."

I didn't know how to be any more careful than I was being. I pushed the curtain back and stepped through.

"Surprise!"

I stopped dead and slammed my hand over my racing heart. My mouth dropped open. Everyone I loved stood there: Will, Angelica, Mum, Liv, Beren, Sarah, James, Millicent with Annabelle in her arms, Lavender, and even Phillip, who I didn't love, but he was okay.

Imani put a hand on my back. "So, love, Angelica was kidding this afternoon. We're not going back to Westerham just yet."

Will stepped up to me. "First of all, we're going to Australia for a two-week holiday and a wedding." He grinned.

This time, when the tears burnt my eyes, I let them fall.

"You guys suck! But I love you anyway." I laughed and looked at Mum. "We're really going home?"

She came up to me and held my hand in both of hers. "Yes, sweetie. It's been a long time for me." Her smile wilted. "I just wish your father could've been here." She sniffled. "But I've missed home, and for better or worse, I'm keen to return. Plus, my only daughter is getting married." Her smile lit up her whole face. "I never thought I'd live to see the day."

I gave her a hug. When we were done, I looked at my loved ones and shook my head. "You guys got me good."

"And you've got us all *for* good." Liv pounced on me. "Group hug!" Everyone crushed in, even Angelica.

I was finally going home.

Book 20 in the PIB series will be out 19th March, 2023.

In the meantime, if you'd like to try my ghost cosy mystery series—Haunting Avery Winters—you can order book 1, A Killer Welcome, online or from your local bookstore.

Avery Winters was overjoyed to be brought back to life... unfortunately, the dead were waiting for her.

Aussie journalist Avery Winters was content—she had a caring boyfriend, great job, and supportive... okay, so her parents weren't actually supportive, but she'd accepted she could never be the son they'd wanted seeing as how she was born a girl. Avoiding them seemed to work well, and, she reasoned, no one's life was perfect. And that was fine, except whilst covering a news story in a storm, Avery's cosy life disappeared in a flash. Lightning struck, stopping her heart and blowing her favourite black boots to smithereens. It was pure luck that an off-duty nurse was walking nearby.

When Avery came to in the ambulance en route to hospital, she'd thought the worst was over. She was wrong. Her lightning-induced hallucinations—there was no way they were ghosts—were impossible to hide. Her boyfriend soon left, and her boss suggested she take extended leave. Unable to cover her rent, she moved back in with her parents. And that's when the fun really began. Unable to cope with their insistence she was crazy, and desperate for an escape, she responded to a journalist-wanted ad... in the UK, because getting mega far away from her parents could only be a good thing.

Armed with a new fear of storms, companions others couldn't

see, and the hope that leaving the stress behind would improve her mental state, she boarded a plane for London. What she didn't count on was not being able to leave her ghosts behind… literally.

Oh, and that the quaint English village she'd be living in had more skeletons in its closet than the Natural History Museum. When she stumbles upon a dead body in her rented apartment on her first day, she's tempted to get back on the plane. But whilst it's not a good omen, returning to her parents would be worse, so she decides to stay.

Only, she's not sure if it's the best decision she's ever made, or the worst. She's about to find out.

ALSO BY DIONNE LISTER

Paranormal Investigation Bureau

Witchnapped in Westerham #1

Witch Swindled in Westerham #2

Witch Undercover in Westerham #3

Witchslapped in Westerham #4

Witch Silenced in Westerham #5

Killer Witch in Westerham #6

Witch Haunted in Westerham #7

Witch Oracle in Westerham #8

Witchbotched in Westerham #9

Witch Cursed in Westerham #10

Witch Heist in Westerham #11

Witch Burglar in Westerham #12

Vampire Witch in Westerham #13

Witch War in Westerham #14

Westerham Witches and a Venetian Vendetta #15

Witch Nemesis in Westerham #16

Witch Catastrophe in Westerham #17

Witch Karma in Westerham Book #18

Witch Showdown in Westerham Book #19

Book #20 (coming March 2023)

Christmissing in Westerham (Christmas novella)

Haunting Avery Winters

(Paranormal Cosy Mystery)

A Killer Welcome #1

A Regrettable Roast #2

A Fallow Grave #3

A Frozen Stiff #4

A Deadly Drive-by #5 (Coming early 2023)

The Circle of Talia

(YA Epic Fantasy)

Shadows of the Realm

A Time of Darkness

Realm of Blood and Fire

The Rose of Nerine

(Epic Fantasy)

Tempering the Rose

Forging the Rose

ABOUT THE AUTHOR

USA Today bestselling author, Dionne Lister is a Sydneysider with a degree in creative writing and two Siamese cats. Daydreaming has always been her passion, so writing was a natural progression from staring out the window in primary school, and being an author was a dream she held since childhood.

Unfortunately, writing was only a hobby while Dionne worked as a property valuer in Sydney, until her mid-thirties when she returned to study and completed her creative writing degree. Since then, she has indulged her passion for writing while raising two children with her husband. Her books have attracted praise from Apple iBooks and have reached #1 on Amazon and iBooks charts worldwide, frequently occupying top 100 lists in fantasy and mystery.